Everyday Friends

Everyday Friends

Lucy Diggs

Atheneum   NEW YORK   1986

Library of Congress Cataloging-in-Publication Data

Diggs, Lucy.
    Everyday friends.

    SUMMARY: Overshadowed by her accomplished older
sister, thirteen-year-old Marcy feels insecure and
incapable of sticking to any project or activity until
she meets thirteen-year-old Natasha, an accomplished
horsewoman, and determines to learn to ride herself.
    [1. Horses—Fiction.   2. Self-confidence—Fiction.
3. Horse shows—Fiction.   4. Friendship—Fiction]
I. Title.
PZ7.D5765Ev 1986   [Fic]   85-22925
ISBN 0-689-31197-4

Published simultaneously in Canada by
Collier Macmillan Canada, Inc.
Composition by Maryland Linotype, Baltimore, Maryland
Printed and bound by Fairfield Graphics, Fairfield,
Pennsylvania
Designed by Felicia Bond
First Edition

For Ellen Bass, with love

I SHOULD LIKE TO THANK the following people who have read all or parts of the manuscript and have given encouragement, support and many helpful comments: my sister, Elizabeth Diggs, and Emily McCully; Betty Hodson; Jill Jeffery and Faline Ginghofer; the members of the Saturday Group: Marilyn Wallace, Elizabeth Stewart, Joan Cupples, Katy Supinski, Caroline Fairless and Kermit Sheets; the women in Ellen Bass's Santa Cruz writing workshops, too numerous to name, but remembered and appreciated. To Lucie Wharton and the riders at Whileaway Farm for valuable information about the horse world, to David Tresan for being steadfast, and to Ellen Bass for the title.

Friend,
My horse
Flies like a bird
As it runs.

Chapter 1

MARCY'S EYES WERE looking at the equation Mr. Thompson had written on the blackboard, but they were doing that thing they sometimes did when she let them. She called it fuzzing out. If she looked at something for a while it would unfocus, become transparent, like a window, and even though the thing itself was still there in the foreground, beyond could be almost anything: a vast empty space like the sky or the ocean, or a geometric design that launched into motion, red whirling into pink, pink swirling into orange, and then . . .

"Marcy? z equals what?" Mr. Thompson was tapping his finger against the chalk in exasperation.

Marcy forced her eyes to focus on the equation

while her neck prickled with anxiety. She had no idea what any of it meant, let alone z. She glanced quickly at Susan who was sitting one desk over. Susan had always been better at math than she was. Marcy could depend on her to whisper the answer and bail her out. But Susan was bent over her math book, and her hair, which had grown longer over the summer, fell across the side of her face like a curtain. Marcy tried to get her to look up by concentrating and repeating a silent incantation: *look at me, Susan. Look at me, Susan. Sue, I need you to tell me the answer*. Susan's head stayed bent. Marcy guessed.

"Ten?"

The class roared with laughter. Mr. Thompson laid the chalk on the tray and rubbed his fingers together to get rid of the chalk dust. "I don't think you've heard a word I said."

Marcy wanted to say, "Right. Those xs and ys and zs are pretty silly," but she knew that would get her into trouble. On the first day of school, with a new teacher, that didn't seem like a good idea. "I don't understand it," she said. "Could you explain again about the x and y. Y equals what?" This was a technique she'd learned from her father, who was in real estate. He said if you didn't know the answer to a question the best thing to do was ask another question. Offense is the best defense.

Mr. Thompson glanced at the clock. "I don't have time to explain it again now. See me after class. Z equals what? Anyone?"

Several people called out the answer. He smiled. "Right. Very good. Now if you'll all look at the example on the top of page twelve you'll see that what we have here is simply a variation of the equation we just did."

Marcy looked at the example on page twelve and tried to concentrate. A fly buzzed against the window and outside an airplane droned. The letters and numbers in her math book began to wander and weave into chains that meandered across the page like ants.

"All right." Mr. Thompson's voice came from somewhere. "That's it for today."

Books slammed shut, chairs scraped, feet stampeded to the door. The room was empty except for Mr. Thompson and Marcy who stood by his desk jiggling her knee. "Susan can explain it to me," she said. "I don't have time now. I, uh, I have a piano lesson. If I don't get going right now, I'll be late." Merely a white lie. She did have a piano lesson after school, but on Wednesday. This was Tuesday.

"You should have thought of that when you were sitting in class daydreaming," he said. "Now, if you'll open your book to page ten I'll go over the example again with you."

"Please," Marcy said. "Gene—my piano teacher— gets really mad if I'm late."

"All right," he said, "I'll let you go today, but I would appreciate it if you paid more attention in class."

"Oh, thanks," she said, "I'll try," and was out the door before he could say anything else.

Outside Marcy spotted Susan in a group drifting slowly toward the bicycle rack at the edge of the playground. "Hey, Sue," she called, "wait up!"

Susan stopped and Marcy hurried to catch up. "Algebra," she said, "ugh. If you'll help me with the homework, I'll tell you a great idea I have for the English composition, okay?" Susan was good at math, but Marcy was better at ideas. So they helped each other out. "So what if Old Ronzo assigned such a stupid topic, 'What I Did Last Summer,'" Marcy mimicked. "See, what I thought is that we should make up something instead of saying what we really did. We could say that we went to Alaska, or . . . I know! We could say that we stayed home and got a visitation from creatures out of the fifth dimension. Little purple beings with eyes that shine in the dark so they don't need electricity. They can even turn their eyes up to high and cook stuff with them, and . . ."

Susan tossed her head in a way that made her hair flip from front to back. "I already started mine during study hall," she said. "'Being on the Swim Team During a Drought.' I went through three bathing suits and look what it did to my hair." She stroked her hair and bent her head so Marcy could see the part. Her dishwater blonde hair had acquired a greenish tinge over the summer. "Too much chlorine," Susan went on. "No water for showers."

"Boring," Marcy said. "Everybody's tired of the drought. 'The worst drought in California history.' It's been saying that in the paper practically every day all summer."

Susan replied with a cool stare. They'd practiced it often, staring at themselves in the mirror, and then at each other, trying to look sophisticated. But always before they'd done it in the context of a game, their game, and in private. Something was wrong. Marcy's skin prickled, and suddenly she wanted to check herself in a mirror. Did she have a booger on her cheek? A shred of lettuce stuck in her teeth?

"Well, uh, how about the math? I told Mr. Thompson you'd explain it to me."

"Call me tonight," Susan said, moving again toward the bicycle rack. "I've got to go now."

"Where to? I thought . . . I thought maybe you could come over."

"Cho's," Susan said, bending to unlock her bicycle.

Just then Virginia Vose came up. "Hi, Sue," she said, "thanks for waiting. Ready?"

Susan nodded and slipped her bicycle lock into her backpack.

Virginia turned to Marcy. "Oh, hi, Marcy," she said with an elaborate expression of surprise. "Want to come?" It was a challenge, not an invitation.

"No. I, uh, have work to do. Practice," Marcy bumbled out. "I've got an audition coming up." And then she was walking away very fast. She wasn't going to wait around and be humiliated any more. She could feel eyes at her back, everyone watching as she walked down the street alone, and she applied all of her will-power to keep from looking back.

When she turned the corner onto Locust Street she took off her shoes because they made her feet feel like they were trapped. The sidewalk had been soaking in the sun all day, but Marcy's feet were so calloused she could walk along it without flinching, like a Bedouin in the desert striding over the hot sand, swirling her robes around her.

Behind her she heard voices chattering and laughing. A quick look over her shoulder told her that it was Susan and Virginia. She sidled into a hedge quickly enough to escape notice and watched as they pedaled slowly up on their bicycles, the spokes glinting in the sun. They sat up straight, hands resting on the tops of their handlebars. They'd pedal a half stroke, then coast, talking to each other, glancing behind them as if they were expecting something.

"Here they come!" Virginia said. "Let's go!" She and Susan bent into a racing crouch and pedaled faster.

Tad Price and John Jacobs came swooping down the street after them, and when they were abreast of the two girls they reared their bikes up into wheelies and cruised past, grinning.

Cho's, Marcy thought. Last year she and Susan had gone in there once, trying to find out what the attraction was for the crowd that gathered there in the afternoons after school. The sign outside said "Cho's Laundromat," but inside there was only one washing machine and a dryer covered with dust near the cash register. Light came in a sheet through the plate glass window in front, stopping near Cho who sat at the counter behind the cash register, making change, selling bags of potato chips and pretzels, while his wife stood next to him running the Slurpy machine. The cavernous back of the room was cluttered with a few old-fashioned pinball machines, a broken jukebox and video games, flashing eerily in the dimness.

When she and Susan walked in no one exactly stopped and stared at them, but there was a subtle change in the noise level and the activity. No one spoke to them, though they knew almost everybody there. She and Susan tried one of the games. It winked and beeped at them, then said, "You Lose. Try Again" in fluorescent, pulsating green before they'd figured out what they were supposed to do. They bought a grape slurpy with two straws and left.

"Whew," Susan said when they were outside. "I'm never going in there again."

"Me neither," Marcy agreed. "Enemy territory."

So they went up to the water district where they'd roamed for years. They knew all the trails and had a cave that they called theirs. They kept a cache in the cave—some candle ends, a canteen of water, chalk, an old army blanket. On rainy days they'd sit with their backs against the wall watching the rain outside and the fog creeping up the valley turning all the green to gray. Against the background of dripping rain they'd tell each other stories. Marcy would start with, "Once upon a time," then when the story wound around to a place where a crucial decision had to be made she'd throw in an "and," and it would be Susan's turn.

Marcy kicked at the ground with her toe. Dust rose up in puffs and settled in streaks on the top of her foot. If someone had told her what she'd just seen with her own eyes she wouldn't have believed them. Susan going to Cho's. With Virginia Vose. Susan, who'd been her best friend ever since fourth grade. "Judas," she muttered. "Traitor." Then she twirled around three times with her eyes closed and her arms stretched out like wings. This was to change the way she was feeling. It usually worked, but today when she opened her eyes she felt just the same. Lonely. And furious.

Chapter 2

MARCY WALKED ON. From an open window came
the sound of someone practicing the piano, working on
an exercise from Hanon. Marcy slowed down, then
stopped. The pianist kept getting snarled up at the place
where number three crossed over thumb. *Thunk* went
number three on the key. You're playing it too fast,
Marcy thought. You'll never get it that way. She ought
to be practicing herself she supposed. She was going to
audition for the San Francisco Youth Orchestra on No-
vember twentieth. Hardly three months away. Not very
much time, considering the pieces she had to play.

   She decided to tell her mother and Gene that she
wasn't going to do it. It was their idea anyway. She

shifted her backpack onto the other shoulder and set off down the street again. It wouldn't work, she knew it. "I don't understand it," her mother would say—they'd had this conversation before—"a person with your talent." "But I don't *want* to play the piano," Marcy's script went. "It's not a question of wanting. It's a question of discipline. Look at how Dana works at her dancing. You don't get something for nothing, you know."

Marcy though that it *was* a question of wanting—dance was all her older sister, Dana, had ever wanted to do. Every afternoon after school she went to dance class and when she came home she'd do pliés in the kitchen, bourrées down the hall. She read *Dance Magazine* and talked to her friends from ballet class on the telephone. Day after day, year after year. Then last spring she'd auditioned for the School of American Ballet in New York, and she'd been accepted. And a few weeks after that, off she went to New York.

All summer she'd been sending letters on the lavender stationery Marcy had given her for a going-away present. Letters full of talk about the school. Sometimes she even included the combinations she did in class, every step, together with comments on how she'd executed them, and what her teachers said.

After she'd read her last letter Marcy said, "Doesn't she ever think about anything else? She's going to turn into a shoe if she doesn't watch out."

"That'll do," her mother said. "Dana at least has direction, application. She knows what she wants and she's willing to work to get it—work hard." She didn't continue with the other half of this speech, but Marcy knew what it was. It went like this: If you want something all you have to do is go out and get it. But things do not get presented on silver platters. You have to make a decision and then work for it. And the only thing that can hurt you is yourself. Changing your mind, quitting, not working.

Marcy did not love this speech. She'd heard it when she quit gymnastics. She'd heard it when she quit ballet. She heard it every time she broached the subject of quitting the piano. But the thing was, what was the point of doing something if you didn't like it? And how would you know what you liked if you didn't try it? Sometimes she wished she was as sure of herself as Dana was.

"Have you ever thought about doing anything else, Dee?" she'd once asked her sister.

"What else is there to do?" Dana asked in reply.

And Marcy thought she probably never had thought about doing anything else. Dana was a dancer. That was a fact, in the same category as: The rivers run to the sea; the sun rises in the east.

Marcy ran up the front steps of her house and let the screen door bang behind her.

"That you, Marcy?" her mother called from the kitchen.

"Nooo," Marcy said in a high falsetto, "it's a purple person from the fifth dimension with horns and a voracious appetite for pianos." She bent into a crouch and crooked her fingers over her head to simulate horns. "Got any pianos, Mrs. Connolly?" she asked, darting her eyes this way and that, and swivelling quickly on her heels at the same time.

Her mother laughed. "Not for eating. But I do have some bread dough. Do you know how to knead?"

"I never do anything like that. I don't make things, just eat them."

"Well, did you see my daughter, Marcy, as you came along? Dark curly hair, glasses, nice smile? She's a champion kneader."

"No, I didn't. I saw a grumbledy grouchy girl with no shoes and a blue backpack. You wouldn't be talking about *her*, would you?"

"Could be," her mother said, "but she's not usually grumbledy grouchy. Something bad happen today?"

"Not really," Marcy said with a sigh, dumping her backpack on the floor in the hall.

"Well, come on out to the kitchen and tell me about it. PTA bake sale tomorrow."

Marcy flexed her biceps as she followed her mother back to the kitchen. She liked to knead and in Indian wrestling she could beat everybody in the eighth grade except Eddie Wallace, but he was huge. He'd had to lose fifteen pounds so he could play Pop Warner football. She floured up her hands and started in on the dough. As the dough became more elastic she pushed hard against it with the heels of her hands, again and again, push and push. The dough seemed alive, springing back and fighting against her as she worked, but gradually she won and the dough flattened out into a smooth oval.

Then she folded it over, began the flattening process again.

While Marcy kneaded, her mother stood at the sink washing the dough hooks and the mixing bowl.

"Where's Susan?" she asked.

Marcy gathered the dough up into a ball and punched it with her fist, a good sock right in the middle of its face, pretending that it was Susan. "How should I know?"

Her mother set the mixing bowl into the dish rack and turned around. "She wasn't at school?"

"Yes, she was at school!" Marcy almost shouted.

"Some kind of trouble between you?"

Marcy punched at the dough again. "No," she said casually. She had to be careful what she said to her mother about Susan. She and Susan's mother, Estelle, were friends and they compared notes all the time. "She, uh, well, they asked me to go down to Cho's, but they just hang around down there in the dark while the machines go beep and burp and eat your money. 'Meep, murp,' " she mimicked, trying to sound electronic.

Her mother laughed.

"It's not funny!"

"I see."

"Do you, Mom? Do you know what it's like to have your best friend go down to that place with Virginia Vomit? And be all alone with no one to talk to?"

"I think so," her mother said gently. "Lonely. And sad. Maybe a little bit angry too?"

Marcy's throat closed up, and to her surprise she felt tears welling up. Just when she thought her mother didn't understand her at all she'd say something like that. She'd thought she was going to give her a lecture about how she'd understand it when she was older—that was one of her favorites—or that she shouldn't get so emotional over trifles. She ducked her head, swiped at her eyes with the back of her hand and took a deep breath. "But I don't know what to *do*."

"Sometimes there isn't anything you can do. Just go on with your own life." She took a dish towel and started drying the dishes from the dish rack. Marcy turned back to the bread.

"Maybe it's a passing fancy," her mother said after a while.

"No, it's not," Marcy said. "This summer while we were at the lake they were on the swim team together. Now they're thick as that." She held up her hand with her first two fingers crossed together. "And Virginia's even gotten her wearing eyeshadow. Purple. You should have seen her today. Makeup smeared all over her face like a clown. At lunch they were going on and on about blush and stuff. But I think it was just to cover up the zits. Three big fat ones on her chin. It didn't work though, because I saw them, so I bet everyone else did too."

"You should be glad to have such a nice complexion."

"I am," Marcy said, but she wasn't feeling glad at all. "I thought eighth grade was going to be fun, but so far it's the worst year of my life. Why'd we have to come back from the lake anyway? We could have stayed up there, watched the leaves turning in the fall, feel the air get crisp, and when it started to snow we wouldn't shovel the walk or anything, just watch the snow coming down, let it pile up against the windows higher and higher so it would get sort of dim and cozy, like a snow cave. We'd sit around by the fire, pop popcorn and toast marshmallows . . ."

Her mother gave her the you're-dreaming-again look, and Marcy said, "No?"

Her mother shook her head. "Well, the good news is that you can take advantage of the extra time by practicing more. That Beethoven sonata could use some work."

Now this was more what she expected. She thought that practicing more was part of the bad news. "It's too hot," she groused.

Her mother gave her a warning look and Marcy went off to the living room and sat down at the piano. Gene would want her to play the Beethoven in her lesson and her mother was right. It did need work.

She flexed her fingers and started in on some exercises to warm up before she tried the Beethoven, hoping that it would be one of those days when everything would go out of her head except the music. But the notes snaked across the page like the numbers and symbols in her algebra book and she was sweating so much she'd have to clean the keys with milk when she was through. She was playing by rote, not even thinking about the music while her mind was going *buzz, buzz, buzz*, like a fly, at her other problems. Susan. Algebra.

After about half an hour she finally solved one of them. Her father could help her with her algebra when he came home from work. Why didn't she think of that before? He liked math and he was good at explaining things. So when Susan called, if she called, Marcy'd be cool. She'd say, "Oh well, thanks for offering, but I've already done it. What did you get for number four? That was really hard, wasn't it?"

Chapter 3

MARCY WELCOMED FRIDAY, not because she was looking forward to the weekend, but because she'd made it through the week. She'd made it through four whole days at John Dewey, her old familiar school, which no longer felt familiar. Classes were not so bad, but lunches were a different story.

On Wednesday she sat with Susan and Virginia and some of the rest of their old crowd out of habit, still hoping that it would be like last year when she and Susan had traded lunches and Virginia had sat sometimes with them, sometimes with Julie Jacobson and Harriet McIlhenny. Then Marcy had scarcely noticed. Now she noticed. She started to give Susan two of her mother's delicious chocolate chip cookies, then she realized that Susan had already traded with Virginia for a piece of gingerbread.

On Thursday she considered sitting somewhere else, but the other tables were already filled with people who sat laughing and chattering in closed circles. She plopped down next to Susan and managed to eat half of her sandwich while she listened to them talking about Tad Price's new dirt bike and whether Partytime Rose was a more desirable color of eyeshadow to wear with purple than Fission Fuchsia. When Susan turned to her Marcy tried to look cheerful, almost convinced herself that nothing was wrong.

"Don't bother waiting for me this afternoon," Susan said. "I'm not going to choir practice."

"Gene will not be pleased," Marcy said. "We're going to sing the Britten on Sunday. It's complicated and you'll mess it up if you don't go to practice."

"I'm not going to sing in the choir any more," Susan said, and gave Virginia a look.

Marcy shoved the rest of her sandwich back into her bag, not hungry any more. Ever since fourth grade she and Susan had sung in the choir together. They sat next to each other and made up funny words to the hymns— they'd sing "crock of ages" instead of "rock of ages"— stuff like that—and that made it a lot more fun.

"Tell him I'm not coming," Susan said, "okay?"

"Okay," Marcy said, pushing back her chair. On the way out of the cafeteria she threw the rest of her lunch in the trash and wondered if things would ever change. While she was in the bathroom splashing cold water on her face she realized that things already had changed. Just like her mother said, she and Susan had grown off in different directions. At least Susan had, while Marcy felt that she wasn't growing off in any direction at all, but was simply stuck in the same old place, with her same old self.

On Friday she got a stomach ache during history, the period before lunch, and spent the noon recess in the nurse's room.

After school she didn't wait around. She headed straight out of the schoolgrounds and turned right onto Anderson Lane instead of left onto Locust Street. It was a longer way home, but Locust Street was also the way to Cho's and she didn't want to risk running into anyone from her class on their way there. If they didn't see her walking alone they might think that she was doing something interesting and exciting like, well . . . something interesting and exciting.

After she'd walked three blocks she began to wish that she'd gone down Locust after all. It was too hot to be taking the long way around. Then she remembered the path through the Donaldson property, a shortcut to her house. The back of their house and the side of the Donaldsons's adjoined each other, divided by a stretch of woods and a creek. Up until three years ago she and Dana would cross the creek, then take the path that snaked through the woods at the back of the Donaldson property and emerged onto Anderson Lane. It saved four whole blocks on the way to town. Then Mrs. Donaldson had called her mother, said it was too disturbing to have those kids gallumphing through her property all the time, rooting around in her yard, acting as if it was theirs. What the hell, Marcy said to herself, eyeing the gate wrapped with a padlock and chain. I'll sneak around the house. The old bag will never know.

Years ago, her father said, it had been a large estate, but the main house had burned down in 1949 and most of the land sold off for a subdivision. Now the only things left were a falling-down shed, the old caretaker's house where the Donaldsons lived, and the barn, which had been empty for years. They used to play in it before Mrs. Donaldson kicked them out.

Marcy climbed over the gate and dropped down on the other side, her heart beating fast. She set off through the woods, down the path, which was choked with undergrowth, keeping her eye out for poison oak. Everything else was shriveling and dying in the drought, but not poison oak. Just before the path turned sharply right into the clearing where the barn was, Marcy stopped and reconnoitered. She thought the barn could be seen from the house and she didn't want to get caught. Birds chirped, a squirrel skittered up a tree. Otherwise all was quiet. Then she got a prickly feeling on the back of her neck. Something was different. What?

She turned off the path into the woods, walking as quietly as she could. Dry leaves crackled underfoot, too loud in the afternoon quiet. She crept closer to the clearing by the barn, cocked her head to listen. Someone whistling? She shook her head—just the birds—and edged up to a tree trunk at the edge of the clearing to take a look.

Something was different, all right. Just about *everything* was different. The barn had a new roof, new white paint on the stall doors, a new concrete floor on the breezeway in front of the stalls. A new wooden fence circled the clearing in front of the barn and the clearing had been enlarged, smoothed out, filled with sand to make a ring. Inside the ring a gray horse ambled around among brightly painted jumps.

Marcy took off her glasses and wiped the sweat off with her bandana. When she put them on again the horse was still there, standing in the middle of the ring, swishing his tail. Then she noticed a man wearing an engineer's cap on the far side, nearest the house, painting the fence, whistling between his teeth. Not birds, after all. A tall girl wearing cutoffs and a T-shirt with a unicorn on it came down the path from the house. Who was she? What was she doing there? She didn't look like anyone the Donaldsons would know.

The man set his brush down, pushed his cap back, said something to her. Marcy cupped her hands behind her ears trying to hear, but she was too far away. The girl took a halter from the gatepost, climbed through the fence and put the halter on the horse. She led him out of the ring straight toward Marcy. Marcy crouched lower, tried not to breathe, cursed the fact that she was wearing a blue shirt. She'd been spotted! At the last minute they turned off toward the barn and disappeared from Marcy's line of sight. She sank back with relief. The coast was clear now. She could make a break for her house, run. If they heard her they'd think it was only a deer.

Marcy did not move; she was too curious. The man kept brushing white paint onto the raw wood of the fence. The girl did not reappear. Marcy settled back. She would wait.

A branch snapped behind her. Crack! Marcy jumped and turned. The girl was standing a few feet away from her looking at her with gray-green eyes. Her blond hair swung in a long braid down her back.

"Spying?" she asked.

Marcy looked at the ground, feeling mortified, shuffled her foot in the leaves. "No. I, uh . . . uh . . . What are you doing here, anyway?"

"I live here," said the other. "What are *you* doing here?"

"Just passing through," Marcy said, trying to sound nonchalant, trying to figure out whether she was mad or not. "I live over there on the other side of the creek. You . . . you live here? What happened to the Donaldsons?"

"They moved," the other said matter-of-factly. "You always barge around through other people's property?"

Marcy still couldn't tell whether she was mad or not. "This is a shortcut. It was too hot to go around on the street, so I—"

"No skin off my back. Next time you go spying in

the woods I wouldn't wear blue, though. Worse than red."

"I know," Marcy said. "I hadn't planned to. That your horse? You ever ride him?"

"All the time. Not today, though, because we just got back from a show in Los Angeles last night. After a long trailer ride like that I give him a couple of days off, just turn him out, let him relax. This time he'll get a few more days off than usual, though." She pointed at the bandage on his right ankle. "He grabbed himself in the trailer and it'll take a few days to heal." She talked as she walked toward the barn while Marcy trailed along beside her. "What's your name?"

"Marcy. What's yours?"

"Natasha Jones. Everybody calls me Nat, though, except my mother when she's mad at me." She turned abruptly and stuck out her hand. "Pleased to meet you," she said, grinning. Her smile was friendly and her eyes twinkled.

Marcy smiled back. "Me too," she said, gripping Nat's hand. Her father said a firm handshake was a sign of character.

When Marcy let go Nat whistled. "You're pretty strong. Lift weights?"

"Play the piano. Hope I didn't hurt you."

"Nope," Nat said. "A firm handshake is a sign of character. Know why people shake hands?" Before Marcy could answer she went on. "It's a holdover from primitive times. If your hand is open then the other person knows that you don't have a weapon in it."

"Poison dart," Marcy said, "or a teensy dagger."

"Right. People used to smell each other too." Nat stepped closer, crinkled up her nose and sniffed.

Marcy didn't know what to do, so she decided to smell her too. They snuffed and sniffed each other. Then they both started laughing.

"I guess I know why people stopped doing that," Marcy said.

"Yeah, it's a little silly." Nat stepped back a half-step and gave Marcy a searching look.

Marcy felt uneasy again. Maybe Natasha was mad at her after all for sneaking around on her property. Maybe that smelling business wasn't so funny. Maybe she had BO.

"People are kind of snooty around here," Nat said.

"Oh really?" Marcy's heart sank. Did she think she was snooty?

"Yeah. We've lived here for almost a month and you're the first friendly person I've met. It was getting kind of lonely."

Marcy was relieved. "But you must have met some people at St. Agatha's."

"St. Agatha's?"

"Isn't that where you go to school? Or are you in high school?" She could be, she was tall enough, a good five inches taller than Marcy.

"No, eighth grade. I'm going to John Dewey."

Marcy was getting excited again. They'd be in the same class. "But you haven't been there all week."

"Because I was in L.A., at the show."

"My mother wouldn't let me miss school for a reason like that."

"Mine doesn't care. She says there are more important things in life than school. Broadening experiences. Now let's see . . . I've just got to feed Joey, then maybe you'd like to come up to the house. Get something to drink. Meet Sasha."

"Sure," Marcy said, wondering who Sasha was. Her sister, she guessed. "Does everybody in your family have Russian names?"

"We're Russian. My grandparents were born there." Nat took an armful of hay from one of the bales stacked against the side of the barn and threw it over the half door into her horse's stall.

"Jones isn't Russian."

"My mother's family is Russian. Her name is Tchelitschev. Jones is my father's name, and he . . ." She trailed off as if there was something about her father she didn't want to talk about. "Joey, meet Marcy," Nat said, returning to her matter-of-fact tone. "You can pet him if you want."

Marcy approached gingerly. He'd looked big out in the ring. Up close he was huge. Marcy stuck her hand out toward his face and he stepped back and snorted.

"Quietly," Nat said. "Horses hate sudden movements because they used to be wild. Could be a mountain lion. Right, Joey?" She opened the stall door and stepped inside. "The side's better, see?" She stroked his neck, scratched under his mane.

Marcy reached her hand up and touched his neck, surprised at its softness. She stroked down his neck, moved her hand up and scratched under his mane the way Nat had done. He turned his head toward Marcy and made a soft whuffling noise. Marcy stopped scratching under his mane and held out her hand. He blew on it, his breath warm and moist on the palm of her hand. Although he was so big, he was very gentle and he seemed to be talking to her with his breath. Marcy had always loved animals, but she'd never been able to have one because Dana was allergic. The piny smell of the shavings in his stall mingled with the fresh meadowy smell of the hay and the particular pungent horse smell of Joey, like nothing she'd ever smelled before, drawing her off to a world where cars did not exist, where the streets were filled with horses pulling wagons and carriages, the horses' hooves going *clippity-clop* on the cobblestones . . .

"You can ride him if you want."

"Could I? Could I really?"

"Sure. He's fun. Broke to death."

Marcy stepped back and looked at Joey, assessing him now in a new way, as a horse she might ride, who would carry her along smooth and easy, like . . . like . . . well, she didn't know what it would be like, she'd have to find out. The prospect was exciting—something new and different, something she'd never thought of before. Something that Susan would never do, or Dana either. Dana wasn't even allowed to ride a bicycle because it developed the wrong muscles. "But I don't know how. This is the first horse I've ever even touched."

"My mother'll teach you. She taught me. And a bunch of other kids too. Back in New Jersey she ran the pony club. She likes it, says it's a welcome respite from her work."

NAT PUSHED OPEN the back door of the house and led the way into the kitchen, one end of a big L-shaped room. On the white enamel kitchen table some architectural drawings were laid out. The doors to the cupboard underneath the sink were open and a pair of legs in faded Levi's rolled up to the knees and sandals laced in crisscrosses partway up the calves stuck out from underneath.

"That you, T.C.?" A woman's voice came from underneath the sink.

"No, it's me," Nat said. "And Marcy. She's a neighbor."

"Just a sec. Hand me that wrench, will you?"

Nat turned to the toolbox on the counter and surveyed the contents. "Which one?"

"The pipe wrench with the red handle. This one is too small."

Nat picked the wrench out of the box and handed it down. There were some clanks and grunts, then the rest of the person emerged from underneath the sink—a tall slender woman in a purple cotton shirt with her hair twisted into a knot on top of her head. "Nice to meet you," she said with a smile. Her eyes were the same gray-green as Nat's and her voice had a lilt, maybe some kind of an accent. She put the wrenches back in the toolbox and wiped her hand on a rag. "Old houses like this have character," she said, "but I can't say much for the plumbing."

"How do you do?" Marcy said, trying not to stare. No one's mother she knew dressed like that, and when something was wrong with the pipes in her house, her mother called the plumber. Her hand when Marcy shook it was rough and calloused and Marcy thought she would probably lose if she Indian-wrestled with her.

"She wants you to give her lessons," Nat said, handing Marcy a glass of something brown and cloudy.

"Be glad to," her mother said. "How nice to have a friend nearby."

When she said that about a friend Marcy glanced at Nat. Nat grinned at her and Marcy blushed. She already liked it there. The house felt homey and comfortable, with companionable litter on the kitchen counters; and the red painted chairs at the table were bright and cheery. Her eyes roved to the living room. An apricot-colored sofa sat at one end and on the wall behind hung a large oil painting. A bookcase lining the inner wall was crammed with books, silver vases and trays, brass candlesticks, an intricately carved wooden thing that may have been a puzzle—or was it a sculpture?—a large crystal rock with many points sticking out in different directions and, in between the points, dusts of white as if snow had fallen in the crevices and crystallized there.

Nat turned to Marcy. "Want some more juice?"

Marcy's glass was still full. "What kind is it?" she asked, eyeing the brown cloudy stuff suspiciously.

"Apple."

"Doesn't look like any apple juice I ever saw."

"It's natural."

"The kind my mother gets isn't unnatural, and it doesn't have all that stuff growing in it."

"It's just sediment and pulp. It's better for you because it hasn't been filtered or refined or loaded up with preservatives and crap."

Marcy flicked her eyes sideways at Nat's mother. If she'd said something like that in front of her own mother she'd be in deep trouble, but Nat's mother didn't object. Marcy gave the juice another suspicious look, then drank it down fast, the way she did when she had to drink warm milk. It tasted more like apples than the kind they had at her house.

The man in the engineer's cap who'd been painting the fence came in the front door, at the other end of the living room, shaking his head. "Truck won't start," he said with a drawl. "Reckon I'll have to use yours to jump-start it."

"Sure," Nat's mother said. "Take a look at these plans first. I think I've finally got it solved."

He rolled a cigarette, struck a wooden match with his thumbnail, breathed smoke out. His eyes caught Marcy. "Wal, now, I haven't met this little lady, have I?"

"Oh, sorry. Marcy—what did you say your last name was? Meet T.C.—T.C. Edwards."

T.C. gave her a wink and lifted his cap. His hair was gray and curly and his eyes were pale blue and squinty around the corners as if he'd spent years working out in the sun.

Marcy bobbed her head. "Connolly."

"It's a pleasure," he said. Then he pointed at the plans with a gnarled tan finger that crooked unnaturally. "You want me to shore up that 'ere wall?"

Nat's mother nodded.

He shook his head. "Be a hell of a lot easier if we just tore it down. Started with some good old new stuff that hadn't been out there rotting for years."

"You can't buy wood with a patina like that. It'll be gorgeous."

"Well, I ain't no artist," he said, then squinted at the drawing, counted on his fingers. "Well, ten four bys oughta do it. I could get started on Monday if they got the lumber in stock . . ."

Nat held up the bottle of apple juice and looked at Marcy inquiringly. Marcy shook her head. Nat gestured toward the living room and Marcy followed her out of the kitchen. In the living room Marcy stopped to look at the painting behind the sofa, a swirl of colors and patterns, nothing she could recognize.

"Like it?" Nat asked.

Marcy hesitated. Her mother said if you couldn't say something nice then you shouldn't say anything at all. She thought maybe it was a trick question, some kind of a test. "I, uh, well," and then the words came out, not the noncommittal ones she'd planned: "Looks like someone dribbled paint all over the canvas and smeared it around with their feet."

Nat whooped with laughter. "I think so too. I like paintings with something you can identify in them, but

Daniel says representational art is as dead as dinosaurs. This expresses the chaos of the universe. The final nihilistic impulse of the human race."

"Sure," Marcy said, making a mental note to look up "nihilistic." "Who's Daniel?"

"He's one of Sasha's boyfriends. Was," she corrected herself with an edge to her voice.

Marcy didn't want Nat to think she was stupid, but she was really curious to know who Sasha was. "Who's Sasha?" she ventured.

"My mother."

"Oh," Marcy said, feeling stupid, after all. She knew people who called their mother "Mother," and Susan sometimes called hers, "Ma," when they were kidding around, but she'd never met anyone who called her mother by her name. She sank onto the couch, wondering what else would be revealed in this house which had seemed so ordinary when the Donaldsons lived there, but was now taking on an exotic quality.

"You mean you never heard of her? Sasha Tchelitschev-Jones? She's a famous sculptor."

Marcy shook her head. "No, but art and stuff, I don't know much about it."

Nat sniffed. "That's what she and T.C. are talking about. He's going to make that old shed into a studio. She's got an appointment here at the Art Institute and a deal with the Pentacle Gallery in San Francisco. That's why we moved here from New York. I know you've heard of that."

"Well, sure. My sister's there now. Studying ballet."

"Not New York. The Pentacle Gallery."

Marcy was tired of appearing so ignorant. "Oh sure," she said. "The Pentacle Gallery. Wow. Is your father famous too?"

"I don't know. I never met him."

"Never *met* him!" Marcy squeaked. Nat looked away, silent.

"Don't you want to know him?" Marcy continued, trying to smooth over her blunder, and trying to imagine what it would be like to have a father you'd never met.

Nat looked suddenly disconnected, as if she weren't there in her living room at all, but some other place very far away. "Sometimes," she began in a dreamy voice, "sometimes . . ." Then she shook her head and said in her normal voice, "Nope. Sasha says he's a no-good bum and I'm lucky he's not around." Then she turned and took a smooth polished stone off the bookcase, turned it around and around in her hands, keeping her head bent so Marcy couldn't see her face.

Chapter 4

ON SATURDAY MORNING instead of sleeping in the way she usually did, Marcy woke up early, her head full of fragments of dreams, all of them with horses in them somewhere: She was riding two snow-white horses in the circus, one foot on the back of each, while in front of her Nat rode two coal-black ones. The plumes on their heads bobbed and floated as they circled around the ring and the spotlights, deep rose and brilliant blue, played across their backs . . .

WHEN MARCY ARRIVED at the barn Nat had finished mucking out Joey's stall and was putting away the wheelbarrow and pitchfork. "That's the bad part," she said, "now comes the good part. 'Course riding is even better, but this is good enough." She took a halter from the hook outside his stall, put it on him and led him outside. The sunlight played on the dapples of his coat, prettier than the horses in Marcy's dream. "He needs to be walked," Nat said, walking as she talked, "so he doesn't stock up." That meant his legs filling with fluid from too much standing. It was the first in a long string of words Marcy added to her vocabulary that day.

"Can I do it?" Marcy asked.

"Sure, I'd love some help." Nat handed the lead shank to Marcy and Marcy took it in both hands as if it were a fishing pole. Nat said one hand would do—her right near the halter and her left holding the other end of the rope.

Marcy stood poised, looking nervously at Joey, "Now what?"

"Just walk."

It couldn't be as simple as that, Marcy thought, sure that she would need to coax him or give a secret signal of some kind.

"Just walk forward," Nat repeated, "he'll come."

Marcy turned and walked forward, trying to imitate Nat's casual manner, convinced he wouldn't budge. But when she moved, Joey came right along. She walked down to the end of the barn and stopped. To her surprise he stopped too. Then she walked off again, tried circles and turns. Whatever she did he kept right in step beside her and she felt important as she paraded around with his head bobbing at her side and his feet making small chunking sounds in the dirt.

When Marcy was through walking him, Nat put him in the crossties and showed Marcy how to groom him, taking brushes and currycomb from the tack box and explaining their function, breaking off every now and then to talk to Joey. "You like that, don't you?" she crooned as she scratched his belly. "And Marcy too. He does, you know."

"Do you?" Marcy asked Joey, and he raised his head and lifted his upper lip so his teeth showed. "He's smiling!"

"Kind of," Nat said. "That's what horses do when they meet each other and feel friendly, sort of like, 'Hi, how are you.' "

"And if they don't feel friendly?"

"They pin their ears back, squeal, kick—it can get pretty wild. But you wouldn't do any of those nasty things, would you, Joey?"

When they were through grooming him, Nat put his blanket on him—that was called a sheet—and put him in his stall. Then they went up to the house, still talking. "If they're friends, horses groom each other," Nat said, "that's why they're so easy to domesticate."

Marcy laughed and told Nat about the picture that came into her head of Joey standing on his hind legs wielding a currycomb in one front hoof and a stiff brush in the other.

Nat giggled. "That would be funny, but really they

use their teeth with little scratching motions, and if there are lots of flies they stand head to tail and switch the flies off each other's heads."

It would be nice to be a horse, Marcy thought, and take care of each other like that.

NAT'S ROOM HAD two gabled windows with ribbons Nat had won in horse shows strung above them, a bookcase crammed with books and trophies, and not much furniture—an old beat-up dresser, a honey-colored pine sea chest, and a mattress on the floor strewn with paisley pillows in shades of purple and red. Marcy liked the bright colors and cheery clutter.

On the wall, on a dusky gold background, was a picture of a mysterious-looking man with dreamy eyes and a pointy chin. The other colors were smoky and dark and he held his right hand up, with the fingers extended. In the lower right corner was some writing that Marcy couldn't read.

"What's that?"

"An icon of Saint Demetrius. He saved my grandmother's life."

"A picture?"

"Yes. See, they were traveling across the Ukraine trying to get to the border, to get out of Russia, because my grandmother's family were White Russians and after the Kerensky government fell that was bad news. It took them almost a year because most of the time they had to walk, and they had a terrible time, hardly ever enough to eat, and also some amazing adventures—but, anyway, they finally made it because of good old Demetrius. He was watching out for them."

"Do you really believe that?"

"Why not? My grandmother does. So does Sasha and she's an atheist."

"That doesn't make any sense," Marcy said.

Nat shrugged. "Not everything makes sense." Then with one of the abrupt changes Marcy was getting used to, "Maybe they were just lucky, but I like him anyway."

Marcy liked him too. She stood still in front of the icon looking into his dreamy eyes and began to feel peaceful deep inside, as if it really did have some mysterious power.

"Want some?" Nat asked, holding out a bag of trail mix.

Marcy pulled herself out of the spell of the icon and took a handful. Then she picked up a large blue album from the top of the pine sea chest—Nat's picture album, it turned out. They sat on the floor eating trail mix while Nat showed Marcy pictures of Vince, her first pony, and Sasha with a big black bird perched on her head—that was Jimmy Crackcorn, the pet crow they'd had on the farm in New Jersey. Marcy's favorite picture was one of Joey and Nat jumping a white gate at a horse show. There were flowers in front of the jump and people standing along the rail watching.

"You look kind of grim," Marcy said.

"I was just concentrating," Nat said. "That was a medal class. They get kind of tense. Never mind the expression on my face, you don't get judged on that, but your position and what kind of trip you have."

"Looks like a long way to the ground. Isn't it scary?"

"Nah, that's just a hunter fence. Three feet six. Nothing to it. It's fun, you'll see."

Nothing to it, Marcy thought. Fun. She turned back to the picture of Nat and Joey jumping the white gate, trying to imagine herself instead of Nat on the horse, feeling fluttery inside, the way she did before she played in a piano recital.

Later they went over to her house and Marcy introduced Nat to her parents. They had already heard about her the evening before, when Marcy had come in bubbling with enthusiasm. For once she had some real news—something exciting and different. Her father smiled and said it would be nice for Marcy to have a friend living close by and her mother listened and didn't say much. At the very end Marcy slipped in the part about Nat's horse and that she might want to try riding. Her father said it sounded like fun, which is what she expected. Not only did she look like her father, she also shared his enthusiasm for trying new things. It was her mother she was worried about.

"Seems like you have enough to do as it is," her mother said drily.

"I just want to try it," Marcy said. "The exercise will be good for me, and the fresh air." Her mother was in favor of exercise.

"Might be interesting." That's what she said when

she hadn't decided what she thought yet. Marcy figured she'd hear about it later.

Then she was confident that they would like Nat as much as she did. Now, looking at the Hawaiian print shirt and raggedy cutoffs Nat was wearing, she wasn't so sure. Her mother thought cutoffs were tacky and wouldn't let Marcy wear them outside the house. But she didn't seem to notice. Nat said how-do-you-do politely, in the same way Marcy had been taught, asked for a second piece of her mother's banana bread and admired the garden.

Marcy was pretty sure that they liked her and took Nat upstairs to show her her room, feeling pleased. She thought her room was sort of boring and old-fashioned compared to Nat's, but Nat said she liked it, it had a cozy comfortable feeling to it and she'd always wanted a four-poster bed with a canopy like Marcy's. Marcy looked around at the flowered wallpaper and the carved Victorian bureau and decided that she thought it was cozy too. They found out that they liked the same kind of music, and their favorite books when they were little were *The Little House in the Big Woods* and *Dr. Doolittle*, that they both liked to play Scrabble and hated Monopoly.

"But that stuff in *Dr. Doolittle* about hot water smelling different than cold is a bunch of crap," Nat said.

"Your mother doesn't care if you swear?"

"No. She says it's a great way to express strong feelings."

"I agree," Marcy said, "but my mother doesn't. She says it's not suitable, but other words just don't do it . . . Hey! I know!"

"What?"

"We could make up our own swear words, then I could say really horrible things and she'd never know, Oh! . . ."

"Good idea," Nat said. "My mother doesn't care, but it will be fun to have our own words that nobody else knows."

They each made a list of all the terrible words they could think of. Marcy knew a few and Nat knew some that Marcy had never heard of before. She said she'd learned some good ones from T.C. since they'd moved to California. When their lists were finished they took one letter from each word and put them together to make a new word. It was more fun than playing Scrabble, juggling the vowels and consonants around to make words that sounded real. When they were through, they had five really excellent, powerful swear words, and they re-solved never to reveal their source, but to keep it a secret between the two of them.

ON MONDAY MORNING Marcy stopped off for Nat on the way to school. On the way Marcy told Nat about their teachers. "Old Ronzo Garbanzo is our English teacher," she said. "She's not really old and her name is really Ronnie Robertson, we just call her that. She's into all this touchy-feely stuff and is always asking us what we're *feeling*. 'Course that means we're supposed to feel what she thinks we ought to. If it's something different she gets all huffy and stops talking about how the classroom is a democracy with every single person just as important. She turns back into a regular old bossy teacher and . . ." She went rattling on, glancing at Nat every now and then to see if she was still listening.

Really all her talking about Ronzo was a diversion. She wasn't going to tell Nat what was really on her mind. She was worried about what would happen at school. Maybe, when Nat met the other kids, she'd like them better. There hadn't been anyone new in their class since sixth grade and she would be an attraction.

As they walked down the corridor Nat said, "I'm glad I met you first. I'd be petrified to do this by myself, not know anybody or even what room to go to."

"I'm glad too," Marcy said, "but I didn't know you were scared of anything."

"You'd be surprised," Nat said without elaborating.

When they walked in Susan looked startled, then whispered something to Virginia. Then Old Ronzo gave them a warning look, and they shifted to note-writing. Marcy didn't hear much of what went on during that class, she was too busy speculating about the flurry of notes passing between Susan and Virginia. She wished she had long distance X-ray vision so she could read them.

Then she swore under her breath when Nat swung in with them on the way down the hall to their next class. She should have warned Nat, she thought. You could have, a little voice said inside her. I know, Marcy told the voice crossly. Then she had to admit that she'd done it on purpose; she wanted to see what Nat would do. Well, now you know. First chance, off she goes with *them.*

Their lockers were assigned in alphabetical order, but because Nat had come late she was given a locker at the end of the row, next to Virginia, while Marcy's was up near the beginning, with Susan only two lockers away. Marcy stuffed her English book in her locker, took out her science book and noticed Susan watching her with a calculating look.

When it was lunchtime Nat took her lunch from her locker and said something to Virginia, who giggled in her high-pitched voice and tossed her head affectedly. Marcy walked off down the hall, seething.

She didn't notice that Nat had fallen in beside her until she said, "What's with this Virginia person?"

"I thought you liked her," Marcy said cooly.

Nat put her hands on her hips and stared. "Can I help it if her locker is next to mine? You could do a finger painting in her eye makeup. Ugh."

Marcy gave a forced laugh, which Nat didn't seem to notice. "She asked me to go to Chow's after school," she went on, "but I said I was busy."

"Cho's?"

"Cho's, Chow's, something like that. With video games." Nat turned the corner of her mouth down in disgust. "Those things are worse than TV. Rot your brain. Then she said something about you and . . ."

Marcy got cold and still inside. "What? What did she say?"

"Oh, uh . . ."

"Come on, you've got to tell me."

"She said that last year you were nice, but this year you're stuck-up and snooty and I'd better be careful because you're a real traitor. Turn on your friends for no reason."

"Friends? Them? *I'm* snooty?" This was so ridiculous Marcy almost laughed. Later, maybe, she'd tell Nat the whole story. "Oh, honestly. They win the Snot of the Year Award."

Nat shrugged. "I said you were my friend. A lot friendlier than anyone else I've met here and I didn't want to hear about it. Besides," she said with a mischievous look, "she's not my *type*," she finished, imitating the affected way Virginia talked.

Marcy laughed, for real this time. She thought she was going to enjoy the eighth grade, after all.

Chapter 5

AFTER SCHOOL THEY set off down Locust Street together.

"Come over to my house?" Nat asked.

"I can't," Marcy said, "I've got to practice."

Nat sighed. "I was thinking we could play Scrabble. Or maybe you could explain the algebra. I didn't get it at all."

"I'd like to," Marcy said, amazed that explaining algebra seemed like a desirable thing to do, "but my mother keeps track of the amount of time I practice. She thinks it would be hot if I won that audition."

"Nothing like winning."

"I guess so. I can't get too excited about it, though. It's what my mother wants."

"She's a backstage mother?"

"No, she doesn't go backstage. Not even when Dana is dancing."

Nat laughed and Marcy blushed. "I didn't mean it literally," Nat said. "It's an expression. Means a mother who makes her child do what she really wants to do herself—or wanted to. Never mind what the kid wants. Sasha says it's pernicious."

Marcy put this into the back of her head to think about later. She would also have to look up "pernicious." She wasn't going to ask Nat and risk getting laughed at again.

"You must be pretty good if you're going to audition for something like that."

"I guess. But I'd rather be . . . well, you know—" Marcy broke off, not sure what she'd rather be doing, and caught in the complicated mixture of feelings that her mother and the piano always seemed to constellate.

"Me," Nat said, "I couldn't sit for hours with my fingers in knots over the piano keys. I'd rather be outside riding."

"So would I," Marcy said, suddenly deciding that *that's* what she'd rather be doing.

"Joey's leg will be healed in a few more days," Nat said.

Marcy nodded, then ducked under the fence and scrambled through the creekbed to her own backyard.

While she was sitting at the piano, instead of seeing the pictures the notes often conjured up in her head—a courtly lady in Vienna, twirling and bowing to a Mozart minuet, or Chopin feeling sad and lonely, listening to the rain drip, waiting for his true love to come back from her walk, afraid that she would not—she saw Joey's big, kind eyes and his head nodding gently as he walked. And instead of thinking about tempi and tone, her fingers wandered over the keys while she wondered what it would be like to ride.

MARCY THOUGHT HER life was like a tape recorder a little out of whack—sometimes it would be stuck on pause or even rewind when nothing much happened, or it happened too slowly, then it would speed up as if someone had switched to fast forward and things happened very fast. The week after she met Nat was like that. Besides selling candy to raise money for their school soccer team, there was homework, practicing, of course, a trip to the lumber yard in the back of T.C.'s truck and an opening at a gallery in San Francisco that she went to with Sasha and Nat. There were huge hanging sculptures made out of fabric and bark with pink and blue wire twisted in them, abstract paintings similar to the one in Nat's living room, and more weird people than Marcy had ever seen in her life. She and Nat stood by the food table eating little meatballs on toothpicks and making up stories about the people.

She didn't know whether it was what Nat had told her about riding, the pictures, or Joey himself that made her want to ride so much, but she did know that she did. By Wednesday, when Joey's leg was healed, Marcy was ready. But she had a piano lesson after school, and on Thursday, choir practice. So it was Friday before she had a chance.

Marcy sat on the fence of the ring watching Nat ride. She was getting ready for a show the following weekend and in a few minutes Sasha was going to give her a jumping lesson. Then it would be Marcy's turn. Marcy watched, entranced, as Joey bounded along with smooth elastic strides. She was looking forward to seeing him jump; at the same time she was boiling with impatience, wanting to try it herself.

"What do you think?" Sasha asked, leaning on the rail next to Marcy.

"He . . . he's . . . *beautiful*," Marcy said. Then she stopped. "Beautiful" wasn't a good enough word to describe him. He tugged at her in the way that other beautiful things did—stars winking and glittering in a night sky, or a rose, each petal curled perfectly into the next. But those things weren't quite right either. After all, Joey was alive, and he responded to you, she thought, remembering the way he snuffed her hand and curled his lip and went right along with her when she was leading him.

"He is beautiful," Sasha agreed. "Sounds like you're snakebit already."

"What?"

"Oh, that's just an expression. Means it's something you probably won't get over in a hurry."

"But I don't want to. I love him already. I . . . he . . ."

Sasha nodded and smiled. "I know, believe me." She put one foot on the rail and called directions to Nat, then turned to Marcy and explained what she was doing. The trot was a two-beat gait, she said, pointing out how Joey's legs moved in diagonal pairs, and the canter a three. That made sense to Marcy—a march and a waltz. At the trot Nat's braid bobbed up and down as she posted to the rhythm, and when she cantered it swung from side to side, along with Joey's tail, like a lazy pendulum. Marcy watched and listened, putting Joey's movements together with Sasha's words, feeling more and more excited. Soon it would be her turn. She'd be riding herself!

"Now comes the best part," Sasha said as she climbed through the fence into the ring.

She constructed a jump with two long poles, putting one end of each in the cup on a jump standard and the other end on the ground, so the two poles crossed in the middle to make an X.

"Okay, Nat," she said, "trot the X."

Nat straightened in the saddle, pushed down on her hard hat to make sure it was secure, then trotted toward the jump. Marcy bent forward, tight with anticipation as they approached the jump, then grinned as Joey hopped over the X and cantered away. Sasha was right. It was the best part, so far. After she'd trotted the X a few more times Sasha told Nat to trot a small vertical fence and then canter down to an oxer—a spread fence—several yards away from the first jump. Afterwards she went on around the ring cantering the fences Sasha named, while Marcy watched, enthralled. It must be like flying she thought. She'd always wanted to fly. Sometimes she dreamed that she could. Off she would go, up through rose-rimmed clouds to the wide blue sky, on and on, skimming through valleys, soaring over mountaintops . . .

"Hi there," came T.C.'s drawly voice at her side. "I just come down to see this little horse jump," he said, rolling a cigarette. He had on the engineer's cap he always wore, a plaid shirt and faded Levi's with a tool belt strapped around his waist.

"I think it's great, don't you?" Marcy asked.

"Not bad," T.C. said. He leaned on the fence, blowing smoke and watching Nat with narrowed eyes. The tools clanked lightly as he moved and the smoke was pungent in the air. "She's got a nice feel and he's a pretty cute horse."

"Cute." Marcy snorted. Cute was for bunny rabbits, not Joey. "He's got fabulous form. See how he rounds his back and uses his head and neck over the jump?" she asked, quoting Nat. When she'd showed her the pictures in her scrapbook Nat had explained that form was important. "And how snappy he is with his knees?"

"If you say so, honey. I never paid no attention to piddly ass details like that. I just did it."

Nat turned the far corner of the ring and was heading toward a plywood panel painted to look like a stone wall when Marcy suddenly had a thought.

"Why does he jump?" she asked. "Why doesn't he just go around the fence? Or stop?"

"Some turkeys'll do that," T.C. said, "but not often with a rider who knows what she's doin', like Nat here. You just gotta keep 'em between your hands and your legs. Let 'em know who's boss."

"It looks pretty exciting," Marcy said.

"Damn tootin'. 'Course this ring stuff is pretty tame potatoes compared to the wide open spaces. When I was workin' at the Lazy Bar B Ranch in Colorado we used to go out huntin' coyotes. Some of the ranchers'd come out all doodadded up in red coats and them fancy top hats, playin' like they was back East somewheres at a lah-de-dah hunt club, but once we got goin' it didn't make no difference what you had on or if you knew the right lingo—callin' red 'pink' and nonsense like that. Shoot, we'd just go hell-bent for leather, galloping more miles in a morning than you could count and jump anything in the way—cricks, bob wire fences, fallen trees big as a house—now *that* was exciting," he said, jabbing the air with his cigarette. " 'Course it's dangerous as hell too. Horse can step in a gopher hole and break a leg quicker'n you can say Jack Robinson."

"But this ring is sand. It doesn't have any holes."

"I know what I know," T.C. said. "You take up jumping you better watch out 'cause you'll run into trouble sooner or later."

Marcy decided that T.C. didn't know what he was talking about. Who ever heard of trees as big as a house? That a horse could jump? Sasha hadn't said anything about trouble, and Joey and Nat were ticking around the ring regular as a metronome. It looked easy as pie.

In the ring Nat had finished jumping and was standing in the center talking to Sasha.

"Well, I reckon that's about it," T.C. said. "Time for me to get back to work. This here's been a drought, but when you got a structure with no roof on it, you can bet your bottom dollar the next thing it'll do is pour cats and dogs." He raised his cap, gave Marcy a wink and moved off down the path toward the house. Marcy watched him go with relief. She thought if he watched her he would make her nervous; she never knew what he was going to say next.

In the ring Nat swung her right leg over the saddle, took her left foot out of the stirrup and vaulted to the ground. "Okay, Marcy, you ready?"

"I'm ready," Marcy said as she jumped off the fence and walked toward them. She was more than ready.

Chapter 6

MARCY STOOD IN the center of the ring beside Sasha and Nat and Joey, so excited she had to command herself to stand still. She didn't want to start out by doing something silly like spooking Joey.

"Okay, Marcy," Sasha said, "your turn."

Marcy grinned. "Ever since the day I first saw him I've wanted to try this. I've even been dreaming about it."

Sasha smiled. "I know. I've felt like that since I was four years old and saw my first horse. It was a fat little chestnut pony just the right size for me. There was something about the sound of his hooves going clippity-clop, the way his tail swished, the way he tossed his head

—well! I couldn't wait to have one of my own." She paused and smiled at Marcy again. "My poor mother. She thought it was a childish whim, something I'd out-grow. Little did she know that thirty years later I'd still feel the same." As she was talking she took a long rope-looking thing with a swivel snap on one end and a loop at the other from where it hung coiled over the post of a jump standard.

"What's that?" Marcy asked.

Sasha doubled the reins over Joey's neck and attached the snap to the bit. "It's called a longe line," she said. "It's a way for me to control Joey from the ground."

"What for? Why can't I ride like Nat did?"

"You will," Sasha said, "but not yet. You have to learn to control your own body before you try to control the horse, and this is the best way to do it. This way I'll control the horse and all you have to worry about is yourself. Okay, now come here and I'll give you a leg up."

Marcy stood beside Sasha, on Joey's left side, her arms stretching up toward his withers. Sasha took Marcy's left leg in her hands and on "three" Marcy sprang, and Sasha gave her a boost. She swung her right leg over the saddle and there she was!

"How does it feel?" Sasha asked.

"Great," Marcy said in a shaky voice. "It's a long way to the ground, though. Are you sure it's safe?"

"Pretty sure. With horses you can't be positive about anything, but he's not silly and Nat's already ridden him."

Marcy put her feet in the stirrups and tried not to

think about how far down the ground was. Sasha showed her the correct position for her legs and told her to fold her arms over her chest. "That's the way to develop an independent seat," she said. "It's important that you learn to balance without using your hands. Okay, ready?"

Marcy nodded, secretly wishing that she had something to hold on to. She knew a Western saddle had a high cantle in the back a rider could lean against, and a horn in front to grab. Even merry-go-round horses had poles to hold onto. But up there on Joey there was nothing but air.

Sasha said "Walk" to Joey and he walked off to the left, circling around her.

"Oh!" Marcy said, "OH!"

"Like it?" Sasha asked.

Marcy nodded. It was the most amazing feeling she'd ever had, gliding along, looking down at the rest of the world, something like being on a bicycle, but better. She felt like a princess in India, high up on an elephant, swaying majestically. She clutched her gold sari around her and smiled down at the mere pedestrians swarming at the elephant's feet . . .

"You look pretty good," Sasha's voice broke in, "but a little stiff. Relax your back. Try to let your hips follow the movement of the horse and get your heels down. That will make you more secure in the saddle."

Joey kept walking in a circle around Sasha as Marcy tried to relax her upper body and get her heels down. It was hard to make one thing tight and the other loose, and with her legs stretched out over Joey's back her heels wanted to go up, not down.

"It's just like ballet," Sasha said, "only in reverse. Point your toes up, and push down with your heels."

Marcy tried that and it helped. She liked the idea of it being the reverse of ballet.

Next Sasha taught her the half-seat. That meant she had to rise up in her stirrups and get her seat out of the saddle. Marcy tried, but she couldn't do it.

"Okay," Sasha said, "grab mane with your hands and use them to help get yourself out of the saddle."

Using her hands, Marcy could do it.

"See," Sasha said, "that's why you want to start on the longe line. If you were holding the reins and had to use your hands for balance you'd be jabbing him in the mouth, and that would hurt him. Horses have sensitive mouths. All right, now practice getting up out of the saddle and sitting back down while I say 'up, down.' That's what you'll have to do when Joey starts to trot."

"Yeah, post," Marcy said, remembering what Sasha had told her while Nat was riding.

Sasha said, "Trot!" to Joey. He started trotting and Marcy lost her balance, bounced around wildly while she clutched at the saddle.

"Grab mane!" Sasha said. "Listen to my voice. Up, down. *Up*, down."

Marcy listened, and soon she stopped bouncing and was able to rise out of the saddle when Sasha said "up." It was more comfortable that way because she was working with the rhythm of Joey's gait instead of against it.

"All right," Sasha said. "Now I want you to let go of the mane. Fold your arms over your chest and see if you can do it without using your hands."

Marcy let go of the mane, lost the rhythm, and found herself bouncing again.

"Marce, push down with your heels. Keep your legs steady—they're your base of support—and let Joey throw you out of the saddle. You're trying too hard. Let him do the work."

Marcy bounced and wobbled, but tried to do what Sasha said, and soon she had the rhythm again. She was posting without using her hands!

I'm better than an Indian princess, she thought. All they do is sit on the elephants under a fancy canopy, but I'm actually *doing* something. I could be an outrider in one of those Indian processions, or a pony express rider, galloping over the plains, over the mountains, through wind and rain and storm . . .

The next thing she knew she was lying on the ground gasping for air.

Sasha stood over her. "Marcy? You okay?"

Marcy looked up at her dazed, wanting to ask what happened, but she could hardly breathe.

"You've had the wind knocked out of you," Sasha said. "You fell off. Just take it easy. Don't gasp. Try to let the air into your lungs slowly."

Marcy obeyed and soon her head stopped spinning

and the tightness in her chest began to dissipate. She sat up and looked around. The scene came into focus. Nat was standing a few yards away, holding Joey, and Sasha was squatting beside Marcy, looking concerned.

"Feel better now?" she asked.

Marcy nodded. "Wh . . . what happened?" she asked. "The last thing I remember I was riding. I was posting, right? Up, down, *up*, down. I was doing that, wasn't I?"

"Yep."

"Well?"

"Well, a deer came running out of the woods just outside the ring and Joey shied and you hit the dirt."

Marcy shook her head. "I don't remember."

"That happens sometimes. The last few seconds before an accident can be a blank. Why don't you try standing up now?"

Marcy just sat there. She didn't want to stand up. She was humiliated. "You said he wouldn't do anything!" she wailed.

"I couldn't take a deer into my calculations. Some things will spook any horse, even a sensible one like Joey. But don't worry, everyone falls off. I couldn't begin to count the number of times I've fallen off. So now you've got your feet wet. You're a rider."

"I sure don't feel like one. I feel like a . . . an incompetent. Or something."

"Well, you're not. Like I said, it happens to everyone. Now, you'd best get up and get on again."

"Get on again?"

"Sure. Don't want to have your first lesson end like that, do you?"

"No. But it did."

"That doesn't have to be the ending. It was just an accident that occurred in the course of the lesson. And if you don't get on again you'll be brooding about it for longer than you should. Come on, I'll give you a leg up and we'll make another ending. You can practice posting some more. You were just getting the hang of it."

Marcy followed Sasha over to where Nat was holding Joey and let her give her a leg up. She was wrestling with a new emotion: fear.

"You're not scared, are you?" Sasha asked.

Marcy shook her head no, thinking that if she was already a failure she might as well be a liar too.

"The only way around it is right through the middle," Sasha said. "Now, up, down, *up*, down, *up*, down."

Try as she might, Marcy could not find the posting rhythm again and slithered and slathered around in the saddle.

"Relax, relax," Sasha said. "Look at Joey's ears. See how he's pinning them back? That means you're irritating him with all that bouncing around."

Marcy clenched her teeth and tried to post, but she kept coming down when Joey was going up. Or something.

"All right," Sasha said after a few minutes. "Maybe you're getting tired. I'll let Joey walk for a few minutes while you take your feet out of the stirrups and shake your legs to relax the muscles."

While Joey circled around Sasha, Marcy relaxed enough to feel the movement of his legs beneath her again. She stifled an impulse to grab hold of his mane. You're worse than an Indian princess, she told herself. Maybe they just sit there under a canopy, but at least they don't fall off.

"That's enough for today," Sasha said. "We'll give it a try again tomorrow, okay?"

"I don't know," Marcy said. "The audition for the Youth Orchestra is coming up soon. I ought to practice, and . . . and . . ."

"And what?"

"It looked like fun when Nat did it. I didn't know it would be so h-h-hard."

"Everything worth doing is hard," Sasha said. "You'll get it, if you want to. But it will take work. Riders are made, not born."

Chapter 7

THE NEXT MORNING Marcy dawdled around the house. She worked on her homework, she practiced the piano, she wandered out into the garden and offered to help her mother set out bulbs. No matter what she did, though, her mind kept wandering over to the barn. She kept seeing Joey, remembering what it was like to be sitting in the saddle and the rhythm of posting when she'd had it. Well, if she could do it once, she could do it again. And she did want to. She called up Sasha and arranged for a lesson the next day.

It wasn't easy, though. In the next few weeks Marcy kept telling herself that riders are made and not born. The way to get to be a good rider was to work. And work and work. Somehow, she hadn't thought it would be so hard. It looked easy when Nat did it, or the cowboys on TV. They sat on their horses as if they belonged there, as if they didn't have to think about things like pushing down with their heels and keeping their backs straight. And they certainly didn't look as if they were *afraid*. Otherwise how could they ride along, with their rifles slung casually over their saddles, doing normal things like talking and laughing, and abnormal things like chasing after bandits and shooting them?

When her mother asked her how the riding was going Marcy answered, "Okay."

Her mother gave her a quizzical look and said, "Anything's hard in the beginning, you know. Remember what it was like when you first started playing the piano? You used to cry you got so frustrated. Remember that Mozart minuet?"

Marcy nodded and made a face. "All those accidentals. Ugh."

"Remember how hard you thought it was?"

She nodded again.

"Well, why don't you get that out and play it now?"

For once she didn't feel like arguing with her mother. She riffled through the stacks of music on the stand until she found the book, *The Easiest Original Mozart Pieces for Piano*. It opened automatically to the piece in question. The page looked dingy from being thumbed so many times.

She set it on the rack and began to play, the notes flowing from her fingers in perfect rhythm. It was a delightful dance—sunny and light as a bowl of oranges gathering in the sun. When she was through her mother clapped, and Marcy smiled with delight. "Thanks, Mom."

"You're welcome."

And Marcy turned back to the piano, playing with a freedom and a confidence she'd never had before.

USUALLY SASHA GAVE her a riding lesson twice a week. The days in between Marcy rode by herself, after Nat rode, practicing the things Sasha'd told her in her lessons. It was like the piano in some pretty awful ways. No matter how many scales she played or finger exercises she did, there was always room for improvement. And when she was working on a piece, no matter how good it sounded, Gene could always find something that needed more work. So with riding: After she learned the posting trot, then she learned the sitting trot, in which she was *not* to post, but sit with her bottom glued to the saddle even though Joey seemed to be trying his best to throw her out of it. Then came cantering and various sorts of turns. And when she'd become reasonably proficient at these things, Sasha announced that she'd have to do it all without stirrups, because that was "the only way to develop an independent seat."

"When can I jump?" Marcy would ask.

"When you're ready."

"I am ready."

"When *I* think you're ready. No sense in trying to run before you know how to walk."

There were times when it was agony, and her body ached so much that Marcy longed to give up, go home and curl up in front of the TV with a bag of potato chips. But she didn't. She didn't want to be a quitter this time. Riding wasn't like gymnastics. It wasn't like dancing either. It was the only Olympic sport that involved another living being; and having to control the horse, to think about what was going on in his mind at the same time she was thinking about what to do with her body, and what was going on in *her* mind, was a new one on Marcy. It was different, and it was a challenge—more difficult than anything she'd ever done before.

Then one day as she was cantering around, she could feel all the parts of her body—her seat in the saddle, her legs firm against Joey's sides, her hands on the reins following his mouth. It didn't feel like work any more.

"What happened to you?" Sasha asked.

"Huh? What do you mean?"

"All of a sudden, today, you look like a different rider. Graceful, easy, as if you're not fighting something any more."

Marcy blushed. "Just work, I guess."

Sasha gave her a contemplative look and Marcy tensed, waiting for a correction. "Okay, you're ready."

"For what?"

"To jump."

"I am? Really?"

Sasha smiled and made an X. "Really. Why don't you try this crossrail?"

"You . . . you . . . mean *jump* it?"

"Sure. Just trot down in your half-seat with your hands up on the crest of Joey's neck. That way you won't jab him in the mouth if you get jostled loose. It's simple. You've seen Nat do it plenty of times."

Marcy lined Joey up on a line with the crossrail while her heart pounded and she tried to ignore the curl of fear in her stomach. But Joey trotted toward it calmly, hopped over the X in a smooth rocking motion, and then they were cantering away on the other side.

"That was *fun!*" she cried.

Sasha laughed, catching her enthusiasm. "Just wait 'til you get to do some bigger fences. It's exhilarating. It really is. Like nothing else," she added in a musing tone of voice.

Marcy wondered why, if she enjoyed it so much, she didn't ride herself anymore, but for the moment she *was* caught up in this ecstasy she'd just discovered. It was like flying! She felt as if she could ride forever, no longer a creature of the earth at all, but one with wings who could soar and sing with the clouds.

After that she lived for the days when she got to jump. She had jumpingitis. She wanted to jump everything in the ring; she wanted to jump every day. But Sasha said, "You know, there's an old saw that says a horse is born with only so many jumps in him, so every time you jump you're lowering the score. Now, I don't know if I believe that or not. But I do know that any horse can get sour from too much jumping, and with Nat riding him too, once a week for you is plenty."

"Oh, phooey," Marcy said. "I want to get better sooner. I want to jump more."

"You will. It would help if you had your own horse."

"I know," Marcy said. "I *want* one. I know it would help a lot. But Mom and Dad say I have to prove I really want a horse. They think I'll quit."

"Looks to me like you *are* proving it," Sasha said.

Whenever Sasha praised her Marcy glowed with pleasure. Every afternoon she worked hard, thinking about how pleased Sasha would be when she saw how much she'd improved.

Then Marcy went to a show with Nat, and when she saw what it was like she wanted to ride in a show too. The other riders gathered along the rail looking at the horse and rider in the ring with tight, focused attention. For the first few rounds of a class they would hold esoteric discussions about strides and turns and lines. Then, after a few rounds, when everyone saw how the course would ride, the mood relaxed until the end of the class when the winners were announced. Then the ribbon-winners led their horses into the ring to pick up their ribbons. Then a new class would start and the tension would mount again.

Marcy was hooked, all right. She wanted to be one of those girls gathered along the rail in boots and breeches and coats and hunt caps, with her horse's reins draped casually over her shoulder. Her horse! If she had a horse she would be able to jump twice a week instead of just once. She could work longer and harder every afternoon, and she would be able to ride with Nat instead of before or after. They could go up to the water district for trail rides, and maybe some weekend Sasha would take their horses in the trailer out to Point Reyes, where they could canter along the beach, laughing when their horses plunged into the foaming waves. *And* she could go to a show! If she had a horse . . .

She kept her parents up to date on her progress. She told them how she was learning to jump combinations and gymnastics—that meant two or more jumps in a line —and soon she'd be ready to do courses. She told them there was room over at Sasha's—three empty stalls, in fact, and if she did her own mucking out and feeding, Sasha said she wouldn't have to pay board. These conversations always ended with Marcy saying, "So can't I have a horse, please?" and her parents saying "We'll see," or "We'll think about it. It's a big commitment, you know." Marcy did not give up, and as the weeks rolled by she thought they were beginning to sound more favorable. But then, maybe that's just what she wanted to think.

THEN, ONE AFTERNOON when Marcy went over to ride, Nat said that Joey had been working too hard and it would be better if Marcy didn't ride him that day.

"Oh, so I can't ride him anymore?"

"I didn't say that. I said he's been working too hard, and it would be better if you didn't ride him *today*."

Marcy bit her lip. "Why is today any different from yesterday?"

Nat buckled the girth and swung into the saddle. "When you get your own horse you'll be able to practice all you want. I don't want Joey getting sour," she said over her shoulder as she headed toward the ring.

Marcy went home, furious. How could Nat be so mean? Some friend she was turning out to be! And how was she going to improve if she couldn't even ride? The first big show of the year was in January. She'd been hoping to ride in that.

Everyone at the show would take notice of Marcy and her beautiful golden mare. The announcer would say, "And first place goes to number thirty-three (three was her lucky number, so thirty-three was even luckier because it had two threes in it), Eldorado, owned and ridden by Marcy Connolly."

Then Marcy would trot into the ring with Ellie, who would arch her neck proudly as if she knew exactly how well she had done. Marcy would collect the blue ribbon and the silver tray, smile graciously at the man handing out the ribbons, and say, "Thank you." He would say "Congratulations! Well done!" Then she would walk out of the ring with the sound of clapping and cheering ringing in her ears . . .

Oh sure! Marcy stopped and kicked at a clod of dirt. She'd never get to a show at all, not with Nat being so mean and selfish.

Chapter 8

WHEN SHE OPENED her back door, tantalizing smells
rushed out to meet her. In the dining room the table was
set for eight, and there was a cut-glass bowl of roses on
the table. Marcy's heart sank. It had all the signs of a
dinner party, and when her mother got embroiled in one
of those she couldn't think about anything else. Sure
enough, she was standing at the stove, stirring a pot of
something, with a white linen dish towel tied around her
waist and the phone cradled in her ear. The telephone
in the kitchen had a long cord on it and her mother carried it around with her, moving it from place to place on
the counter as she cooked. She smiled at Marcy over the

telephone receiver and waved, but her eyes had that absent look she got when she was cooking.

"Sure, I understand," she said into the phone. "That's really too bad. Of course I'm disappointed. I thought . . . well, I guess I'm a matchmaker at heart, and I was sure you would hit it off. It's hard to drag him away from that ranch, he's such a recluse and so much tragedy in his life, but he's just your type, and I was thinking that it was about time you started circulating again. You know . . ."

Marcy sighed and started up the stairs to her room. She was halfway up when her mother called, "Marcy! Will you come here and give me a hand, please?"

Marcy backtracked to the kitchen. "I'm running behind," her mother said. "Let's see . . . there are the crudités, and the sauce, and the dough for the cheese puffs, and . . ."

"I have a problem," Marcy said, "Nat . . ."

"Hm? If you could just do the crudités, it'd be a *big* help."

Marcy gave up. "Okay," she said, taking a knife from the rack. "These?" she asked, pointing to a pile of vegetables by the sink.

"Umhm," her mother said. She swiped her hair from her face with the back of her hand and took a cannister of flour from the cupboard.

"Who's coming?" Marcy asked. If her mother wouldn't listen to her, she might as well listen to her mother.

"The McKeons and the Appelbaums and Jim Ferguson. And Madge Albright was coming, but that was her on the phone just now. She said she threw her back out and can't walk a step, so poor Jim will be odd man out, and the whole purpose of this dinner party was to get the two of them together. It seemed just perfect. Madge divorced—it's about time she stopped brooding and started circulating again—and him a widower. You know, I'm always trying to get him to do things, but it's so hard to pry him away from that ranch, so when he said yes, I was just sure . . ." She rattled on and Marcy let her voice drift in and out of consciousness. The voice she was *really* hearing was Nat's, telling her that she couldn't ride Joey.

". . . if I could just think of someone." Her mother's voice tuned back in again.

"What about Sasha?" Marcy asked.

"What about her?" her mother asked absently, working at the butter and flour in the bowl with the pastry blender. "Could you just hand me the cheese, please? The gruyère, I thought I'd do gruyère instead of cheddar, for a change."

"So you'll be eight," Marcy said. "So Jim won't be the odd man out."

Her mother's hand on the pastry blender stopped. She glanced at Marcy, then went back to working the dough again. "Oh, I hardly think so," she said.

"Well, she's not married either," Marcy said. "And she's a lot more interesting than Madge Albright. There's a whole article about her in *Art News* this month. With pictures of her and some of her sculptures."

"I can't ask her at the last minute," her mother said firmly, making it clear that the subject was closed.

Marcy's cheeks burned. She thought it was a good idea, but it wasn't the first time her mother had implied there was something wrong with Sasha. Her mother said that Sasha was a "Bohemian." Since Marcy didn't know what that meant, she'd looked it up in the dictionary: "A follower of art, literature or other intellectual pursuits, who adopts a mode of life in protest against, or indifference to, the common conventions of society, esp. in social relations."

Sasha didn't dress like anyone else Marcy knew and she didn't act the same either. She didn't do the things that her mother did like Altar Guild and bridge club and PTA. She burned incense and meditated, and sometimes she'd get so absorbed in her work she'd forget what time it was. One time Marcy and Nat had waited and waited out at the barn for Sasha to come and give them a lesson. Finally they'd gone out to the garage, which Sasha was using for a studio until T.C. finished building her real studio. She was standing at the far end of the garage looking at some thick transparent pieces of plastic she had piled up in front of the window, so absorbed she didn't see them come in. When Nat spoke she startled. Then she waved her hand vaguely and turned back to the plastic. "Not today," she said, "I'm on to something here. Can't stop now."

"What was that all about?" Marcy asked when they were outside again.

"Oh, just a creative fit," Nat said. "When she's in one of those there's no point in trying to get her to do anything else."

Marcy thought that Sasha's sculptures were pretty weird, just big blobs of wood and plastic and metal that didn't look like anything identifiable. But just last week some people had come from Chicago and paid thousands of dollars for one, so Marcy guessed that proved that she didn't know much about art.

"Jim's a Bohemian too," Marcy said.

"Honestly, Marcy," her mother said in a tone that held a hint of warning.

Marcy took the fifth carrot and began to peel it. It didn't seem like the right time to tell her mother that over at the Joneses they didn't peel their carrots. Most of the vitamins and minerals were in the peel, Sasha said.

"You can do it," her mother said.

"Do what?"

"Make eight."

"I've got homework to do." That seemed like a good enough explanation, even though the real reason was that grown-up dinner parties were boring. She wasn't going to sit there as if she were invisible and listen to her mother and Estelle Appelbaum yakking all night long.

"This is Friday. You have all weekend to do your homework."

"I know. I just don't feel like it." Marcy glanced uneasily at her mother, hoping the explanation would do. She liked the McKeons and Jim Ferguson, but the Appelbaums, Susan's parents, were another matter. Estelle Appelbaum was bad enough, but her husband, Sam, was worse. He was a dentist, *their* dentist, and Marcy always had the feeling that he was going to open her mouth and start poking around at her teeth. "Tch, tch, been eating candy again, I see. And with braces too," and shake his head grimly as if all her teeth were going to fall out of her head any minute. Marcy hadn't liked them much even when she and Susan were still friends, and now . . .

"Dana would do it," her mother said. "For me."

"But I'm not Dana! And grown-up dinner parties are boring."

"You don't think Jim is."

Marcy blushed, and turned away. "The Appelbaums are."

"Let's not go into that."

"Okay, okay."

"Well, if you really don't want to, it's okay with me," her mother said unexpectedly, "but would you help me until dinner's served? I didn't plan this menu too well—I never should have tried to do a soufflé with this sauce. Too many things at the last minute. *And* these cheese puffs." Her voice rose, ending on a frantic note.

Marcy rolled her eyes. Her mother was a good cook, but she got carried away with all those elaborate French dishes. Marcy thought hamburgers or roast chicken would be just as good and one-tenth the trouble, but her mother said she couldn't serve kiddie food to her friends.

MARCY TOOK A batch of cheese puffs from the oven and carried them into the living room. They had puffed as they were supposed to and were a lovely golden brown. Her mother and Estelle Appelbaum were yakking away as expected, and her father and Ian McKeon and Sam Appelbaum stood by the bay window discussing a new computer stock. Jim Ferguson, in Levi's and hand-tooled cowboy boots, was talking to Jane McKeon. He was the only man Marcy knew who could look elegant in Levi's.

Her mother beckoned her over, and when Marcy had said her hellos and passed the cheese puffs, Estelle Appelbaum said, "Haven't seen much of you lately, Marcy, how have you been?" in a fake-cheerful tone that remainded Marcy a lot of Susan.

Marcy mumbled something and Estelle went right on, "I'm certainly hoping we'll be able to hear you play tonight. Your mother has just been telling me about the audition next week. I'd love to hear you play the Beethoven sonata. Beethoven's such a fine composer! So full of feeling!"

A lot she knows, Marcy thought, and looked questioningly at her mother.

"We'd all enjoy it," her mother said, and elicited a chorus of "Yes, do's" from the other guests. "The next

batch of cheese puffs can wait," her mother said, antici-
pating the excuse Marcy was about to bring up.

Marcy sighed and set the plate of cheese puffs down
on the coffee table. Her hands were already sweating.
She wiped them on her pants and went over to the piano;
she might as well get it over with. She ripped through
the Beethoven as fast as she dared and jumped up as soon
as she was though. But Sam Appelbaum wanted her to
play some Mozart, and then her mother asked her to play
a Chopin nocturne. Marcy was furious. Her mother was
taking advantage of the fact that they had guests to get
her to play the things *she* liked. It just wasn't possible
to rip through a nocturne, though, and Marcy launched
into it, hitting the keys grimly, swearing to herself that
she would not play another thing.

Partway through the piece she caught Jim Ferguson's eye. He was looking both at her and through her,
as if she were some kind of vision. Marcy's fingers froze
on the keys; she looked blankly at the music, had no idea
where she was. She bumbled around for a few measures,
hitting wrong notes, trying desperately to get back into
the piece. Then she found her place, her fingers remembered and began playing the right notes again. Marcy's
eyes were on the music, but she was still seeing Jim's
face.

When the last chord faded away, the room was
hushed. Then a babble of voices broke out, telling her
how well she played, what a pleasure it was to hear her.

Marcy smiled and said the appropriate things, then

grabbed the empty cheese puff plate and escaped to the kitchen. She put another batch of cheese puffs into the oven. Then she sat down at the kitchen table and buried her head in her hands, feeling confused.

"That was lovely, Marcella," a deep voice said.

Jim was standing in the doorway. "Something wrong?" he asked gently.

Marcy nodded yes, not trusting herself to speak.

"Something about the music?"

"No. Yes. Oh, I don't *know*! See, this afternoon Nat wouldn't let me ride Joey and when I came home Mom was talking on the phone and then she started roaring around the kitchen as if this dumb party were the most important thing in the world. And she thinks that my playing the piano is really important. But it's not! I don't *care* about the piano. I just do it because she makes me."

"Could have fooled me," Jim said. "Playing that Chopin, you didn't sound like someone who doesn't care about the piano."

Marcy opened her mouth, then closed it, feeling confused again. "Well, sometimes I do, but just when I feel like it. I hate performing like that—on command, as if I were a . . . a trained seal or something."

"I know what you mean," Jim said. "Parents have expectations. It's hard . . ."

"It's hard to be a child too," Marcy said.

"I know," he said, "I was a child too, you know."

"So was everybody, but they sure don't seem to remember."

"Well, I've had lots of time to reflect," he said with an edge of sadness in his voice. Marcy knew that he had reason to be sad. Three years earlier, his wife and daughter had been killed in a car accident. After that he had given up his law practice in New York and moved out to California, to the ranch where he lived now.

Marcy smiled at him. It made her sad too when he looked like that.

He shook the sadness from his face and said, "Now, Marcella, why don't you tell me about this afternoon? And the riding. I hear that you have a new friend."

He was the only person who called her by her real name. She wouldn't allow anyone else to. In fact, she kept it a secret as much as possible. Ever since kindergarten when the teacher had called, "Marcella Connolly," and everyone had laughed, she'd had her mother write "Marcy" on all the forms. None of the kids at school now knew what her real name was, except Nat. But Jim was different. When she'd first met him he asked her what her real name was and she told him, knowing that he wouldn't laugh. "That's a beautiful name," he said. "Do you mind if I call you Marcella instead of Marcy?" She said that she didn't. When he said it, it didn't sound silly, but sophisticated and serious, as if, someday, she might actually be the elegant and composed person she felt like inside, sometimes. The amazing thing was that he seemed to know it was a secret between them. When other people were around, he called her Marcy.

She started to talk, telling him about Sasha and Nat and riding, and how much she liked it. She talked and talked and Jim listened, sitting quite still, absorbing her words. When she got to what had happened that afternoon her voice rose and she felt angry all over again.

"Sharing a horse must be hard," Jim said.

Marcy nodded vigorously. "It sure is! Like sharing a toothbrush. Whoever heard of that?"

"Sounds like you need one of your own."

"Yeah, but Mom and Dad just keep saying 'we'll see.' " She paused and shrugged. "They think I'll quit."

"Are you going to?"

"No. I've just started, and I *love* it, but they say I've quit other things. Gymnastics. Ballet—" She broke off. Was she really a quitter?

"What about the piano? You haven't quit that."

"Just because Mom won't let me."

"Really?"

"Yes!"

Jim looked at her quizzically, as if he didn't really believe her. Marcy wasn't sure that she believed herself.

"Well, if you want to quit you could always sell the horse, couldn't you?"

"Sure, but I wouldn't. Anyway, I have to get one first."

"It's a coincidence," he said, "but you know the young couple who live in my guest house?"

Marcy nodded. She'd met Tom and Kathy Hannah on her visits to his ranch.

"Kathy wants to sell her horse."

"No kidding?"

"No kidding. Now, I know something about cattle

and next to nothing about horses, but this horse seems like a pretty nice one to me. Maybe you could come and take a look."

"I would love to, but Mom and Dad haven't said yes."

"What's that?" her father asked, appearing in the doorway. "Did I heard someone say 'Dad?' "

Marcy nodded and Jim said, "Marcy and I have just been talking about her new passion. She says she wants a horse."

"She does indeed," her father said, "morning, noon and night."

"Oh, Daddy!"

"Well, maybe just once a day, but *at least* once a day.'

"Now, it's really important, though," Marcy said, "because today Nat said I couldn't ride Joey anymore 'cause he's getting sour—or something."

"What? You can't ride him anymore?"

"Well, that's what she *said*, and it is kind of hard on him being ridden by two people every day. I guess," she added, wondering if it was really true, or if Nat was just being cantankerous. When she'd ridden Joey the day before he'd been his usual cooperative self.

"It *has* been awfully nice of her to share her horse with you, and of Sasha to spend the time helping you."

"I know that, but what am I supposed to do now? Don't you think it would be nice of us to stop sponging off them?" Marcy was pleased with herself for thinking of that one. Her father believed in being independent.

He didn't like to be what he called obligated unnecessarily.

Her father stroked his chin, which is what he did when he was thinking. "Hadn't really thought of that," he said.

"We're getting sort of obligated," Marcy said, "and if I had my own horse Nat and I could ride together, we could go up to the water district, we could go out to Point Reyes and ride on the beach, and . . ." Talking about these possibilities was so exciting that the words spilled out of her mouth faster and faster.

"Slow down," her father said, "use the brakes."

". . . and, and Jim says that Kathy Hannah out at his ranch wants to sell her horse and it's a pretty nice horse and what if somebody else comes along and buys it? It's like a golden opportunity. Fate. Luck. Just when I need a horse really badly, along comes Jim and says there's one just waiting for me, and I don't see how you could be so heartless and cruel—"

"Hang on," Jim said. "I don't know much about horses, you know. Could be a lemon."

"Couldn't I at least go and see?" Marcy asked, turning to her father.

"Feels kind of right," he said. "Tell you what. After this party is over I'll talk to your mother and we'll see what she says, then if—"

"Oh, tidduck," Marcy said. 'Tidduck' was one of their better swear words. "You've said that about ten thousand times."

"Maybe only one thousand," he said, "but this may be the last one—when we really do see."

"Say yes," Marcy said, "say yes."

He smiled and said, "I did just sell the Janes Estate, and this afternoon I drew up an offer on the Talbot house, so it would be a good time for me. Financially, that is. We'll see."

Chapter 9

THE NEXT MORNING when Marcy came down to breakfast the house was strangely silent. Her parents were nowhere to be seen and beside her place lay a pale gray envelope—her mother's stationery. She ripped it open and pulled out a piece of paper. It was a cartoon drawing of a horse with a bushy tail and a big grin on his face. A card hung around his neck that said "For Marcy," and was signed "Love, Mom and Dad," the "Mom" in her mother's neat school-teachery writing, and the "Dad" in her father's spidery scribble.

"Mom! Dad!" she yelled. "Where are you? Really? Is it true? Come out, come out, wherever you are!" She kissed the picture of the horse and twirled round and round, bubbling with happiness. When she was too dizzy to twirl any more, she stopped, and her eyes landed on the door to the pantry. It was closed, which it rarely was. "I spy!" she yelled, and ran to open it. Before she got there, her mother and father walked out, looking almost as happy as she felt.

"Is it true? Can I really?"

"Yes," her mother said, "really."

"Oooooh, thank you, thank you, *thank you!*" Marcy said, kissing first her mother, then her father, then back to her mother again. "Let's go!"

"Where?" her mother asked.

"Out to Jim's. To look at Kathy's horse."

"I'm sorry, Marce, but you know Saturday is a busy day for me," her father said. "I've got an open house at that house over on Laguna, and a couple of meetings later in the afternoon. Tess?"

Her mother shook her head. "I'm on the altar committee this month. I've got to meet Estelle over at church. Maybe tomorrow."

Marcy groaned. "I can't wait a whole day. I'll explode!" She paced around the kitchen, unable to stay in one spot for more than a second or two. "Can't we go today, pleeeze?"

They looked sorry, but they said no.

"Sasha then," Marcy said, "maybe she'll take me."

"She's done an awful lot already," her father said.

"But she likes to look at horses," Marcy said, "she told me that, and, really, it would be better if she went.

This horse could have founder or colic or something horrible, and what would we know?"

"What do you think, Charles?" her mother asked.

"Seems all right," he said. "It would be a good idea to have somebody along who knows something about horses."

Marcy was dialing the phone before the words had settled in the air. She was so excited she forgot that she was mad at Nat; and when Nat said they'd love to go, they'd pick her up at one o'clock, Marcy tore up the stairs and spent an hour putting on shirts and taking them off, trying to decide which one would look best with her new horse. She finally settled on a royal blue one with narrow white stripes and a white collar and cuffs. Blue was the right color, she decided, the color of a first-place ribbon, and her horse would be a blue ribbon winner for sure.

M A R C Y S A T O N her front porch waiting for Sasha and Nat to come and pick her up. Everything was happening just right—Jim knowing about the horse, her parents giving their approval, at last. She was positive this was going to be the horse for her. A bright chestnut mare with a coat like a new copper penny—the horse of her dreams who would carry her off through fields of green velvet under skies of sapphire.

"Hey Marce!" Nat called, banging up the porch steps.

"Huh? What?"

"Let's go."

"Oh, okay," Marcy said. She'd been so involved with visions of her new horse that she hadn't seen them drive up.

In the truck they banged along, past McDonald's, the Jack-in-the-Box, and Foster's Freeze. Past the 7-Eleven, Ted's Arco station, and the round tangerine moon sign of Campolindo Natural Foods Store. On past more stores and gas stations they went until there were more houses than stores, then more trees than houses, then open rolling land dotted with dark blobs of cattle grazing in the distance.

"There it is!" Marcy said.

Sasha braked and turned down a road with a big bay tree on one side and a neat sign saying "Three Springs Ranch" on the other.

"Excited?" she asked, glancing at Marcy.

"You bet!"

The road soon changed from asphalt to dirt, winding through woods and up a steep hill. Then the woods thinned and open fields stretched away from the fences on either side of the road.

"Nice place," Sasha said. "And so green. Must be permanent pasture, but how could he have enough water in this drought?"

"Springs," Marcy said. "That's why it's called Three Springs Ranch. Jim and my dad looked for over a year before they found it. Jim said if he was running cattle he wanted to have plenty of water."

"Lucky," Nat said.

"Smart," Sasha said.

The big white farm house stood at the top of a rise, and behind it lay barns, collecting pens, sheds.

"I guess Jim's not here," Marcy said. "I don't see his truck. Oh well. I hope he told Kathy we were coming."

Sasha stopped by the house and they waited for the barking of the dogs to subside before getting out of the truck.

"This way," Marcy said. "The guest house is around back."

After Marcy introduced Sasha and Nat to Kathy Hannah, Kathy said, "Well, come on, I brought Sugar in this morning so you wouldn't have to wait while I chased her all over the south forty."

"That's her name? Marcy asked. "Sugar?"

"Yeah." Kathy laughed. "It's a little corny, but I was fourteen when I got her and I thought it was perfect. Then. And, oh well, I couldn't change her name. She's always been my little sugar."

Inside the barn Marcy blinked, trying to get her eyes accustomed to the dim light. Kathy took a halter from a hook and opened the stall door. The mare came over and nuzzled Kathy, who spoke to her softly. She led her outside and stood her up on the level ground so they could take a look at her. She wasn't coppery gold at all, but a dull, dark brown without a speck of white on her. She wasn't exactly little, either. When Kathy said she was her little sugar Marcy had pictured a small round mare with a friendly expression and a bright star on her forehead.

"She's getting her winter coat," Kathy explained. "In the summer she's got dapples. Beautiful."

Sasha nodded, looking at the mare with narrowed eyes, walking around to view her from every angle. After this preliminary viewing she started around again, bending down and running her hands down Sugar's legs, feeling the knees, the tendons, the ankles, and picking up her feet. At the off hind ankle she paused and probed.

"What happened here?" she asked.

"An old wire cut. She had it when I got her," Kathy answered. "But I had it X-rayed and it's never given her any trouble."

Sasha got up and walked around to the mare's head where she looked at her eyes and ears and teeth.

"She's twelve, you said?"

"Umhm. I've had her since she was four. Managed to keep her all through college, but now Tom's going to Alaska to work on the pipeline and I've got a job up there with the U.S. Geological Survey. They have horses in Alaska, but the weather's terrible and we're going to be moving around a lot. I've had her so long I hate to part with her, but—" She stopped and shrugged. "So it goes. Been riding long?" she asked, turning to Marcy.

"A few months," Marcy said.

Kathy pursed her lips. "Jim didn't tell me that," she said. "Well, she *might* be all right."

"Is she hot?" Sasha asked.

Marcy put her hand on the mare's neck. "She doesn't feel hot," she said.

Sasha laughed. "Not that kind of hot. Raring-to-go-type hot."

"Nooo," Kathy said. "She's sensitive, though. And she can be marish sometimes."

Sasha nodded. "Well, let's see how she goes."

Kathy took her back to the barn and brought her out again with the saddle and bridle on.

"I've made a sort of ring down in the pasture. It's really just a corner of the pasture I've marked out with boards, but it's the only level piece of ground on the whole ranch big enough to work in," she said, swinging into the saddle. "Follow me."

In the "ring," Kathy worked her in both directions. The mare had looked dull and plain standing still, but when she began to move, even Marcy could see a difference. She carried her head low with a slight arch in her neck and moved with easy rhythmic strides.

"Good mover," Sasha said.

"Yeah, we always did well in the hack classes."

"Where'd you learn to ride?" Sasha asked.

"Here and there. I spent most of my money on her upkeep, so I didn't have much left over for lessons, but I picked up what I could."

"It's a shame you have to give it up. Looks to me like you have a real feel."

"I've always loved it and I know I'll miss it," Kathy answered. "But I'll come back to it. I've got horses in my blood."

Sasha nodded. "Me too."

"Want to see her jump?" Kathy asked.

Sasha said yes, and Kathy started trotting back and forth over a crossrail. Then she cantered a single fence a few times and finished up with a little course.

"Nice," Sasha said.

Kathy gave Sugar a pat. "Is that enough or would you like to see anything else?"

"Could we raise the fences? These are pretty small and it seems easy for her."

"Sure."

Sasha and Nat walked around raising the fences, then Kathy jumped her over the course again.

"She can really use herself," Sasha said.

"Yeah, she's got a lot of talent."

"Well, what do you say, Marce?" Sasha asked. "Want to try her?"

"What do you think?" Marcy asked. She had an image in her mind of a golden dancing mare, delicate, yet strong, lovely as a piece of jewelry, and she couldn't mesh this with the big brown mare in front of her whose long coat was streaked with sweat and whose left ear lopped sideways like a mule's. But she'd heard Sasha's positive comments, and she'd seen the expression on her face when Sugar jumped around over the bigger fences —pleased, and excited too.

"I think you should," Sasha said. "We'll have to look long and hard before we find another horse as nice as this."

"Okay," Marcy said, "here goes."

Sasha gave her a leg up and Marcy set off at a walk. She'd never ridden anywhere except the ring at home and the big pasture made her feel insecure. The mare's ears flicked back and forth as if to say, "Now who is this? What do you want me to do?" Her strides were longer than Joey's, and Marcy tried to get the feel of it, but the mare began to jig. Marcy tightened the reins and thought: Walk, mare. Let's just walk. But instead of settling down, the mare shoved at the bit with impatient tosses of her head and her hooves churned the ground.

"Loosen up," Sasha said, "relax."

This was a new idea. Marcy tried it and Sugar settled back into a nice free-striding walk. She couldn't walk all day, though. The sequence went walk, trot, canter, jump. Marcy glanced around. Sasha and Nat and Kathy were standing in a little knot in the center of the ring watching her and Sugar. Beyond the boards that outlined the ring, the big pasture sloped away, down to a little canyon. A wedge of geese flew overhead, honking, silhouetted against the gray sky, heading south. Marcy gathered up her reins and squeezed with her legs. Sugar shot forward and Marcy was so surprised she fell backward, jabbing the mare in the mouth.

"Not so much leg," Kathy said.

Marcy tried to compose herself, but now she was more anxious than she'd been in the beginning. This time she applied what she thought was *no* leg pressure. Sugar shot forward again, faster than Joey ever did. This time Marcy was prepared and stayed with her. After they trotted around the ring a few times Sugar started going faster and faster. Marcy closed her eyes and clenched her fingers on the reins. Oh *help*, she thought.

"Sit up," Sasha called, "do half-halts."

"What's a half-halt?" Marcy managed to ask.

"Open and close your fingers on the reins as if you were squeezing a rubber ball. And use leg."

"Leg?" How could she use leg when the mare was going too fast already?

"To keep her balanced," Sasha said. "She's getting all strung out on the forehand. You want to have her in a frame between your hands and your legs."

Marcy tried to do what she was told, but Sugar began to toss her head and switch her tail.

"Too much hand!" Sasha called. "Lighten up on the reins."

Marcy was in despair. Too much rein; not enough. Too much leg; not enough. Nothing she did was right. Then Sugar let out a big fart and bounded over the boards of the ring. Marcy lost a stirrup. Sugar kicked up her heels and lit out across the pasture. Marcy crouched low on her neck, clutching mane to keep from falling off. The mare flattened out, ran on and on through the field. Tears streamed out of Marcy's eyes. The loose stirrup slapped back and forth banging at her ankle. Her arms ached.

The next thing she knew, they were standing by the fence in the far corner of the pasture. Sugar was panting and blowing. So was Marcy.

She looked back and saw four figures appear over

the rise. Jim was there too. What a time for him to show up! It was bad enough to have the mare run away with her, but to have Jim see it too was almost more than she could stand. Just yesterday she'd been flapping her big mouth, telling him what a good rider she was getting to be.

"You okay?" Sasha's voice came faintly from the distance.

Marcy couldn't answer. She was shaking all over.

KATHY RODE SUGAR back to the upper end of the pasture and Marcy trudged along on foot, humiliated. "I *tried*," she said.

Sasha put her arm around her. "I know you did."

They said thanks and left Kathy at the barn, sponging off her horse.

"I'm sorry it didn't work out," Jim said as they walked along the path toward Sasha's truck. "I had a feeling this would be the horse for you."

"So did I," Marcy said. "So much for those kinds of feelings."

"Too bad," Sasha said. "Nice horse."

Marcy bit her lip. She felt like such a fool. "Couldn't I try her again at home? It would be different there."

Sasha shook her head. "She's just too much horse for you, Marce. You need something quieter, not so sensitive. If you had a horse like that it would make you scared."

Make me scared, Marcy thought, *make* me scared.

Then what am I already? It was really horrible, too, just when she was getting her confidence on Joey. She wanted to ring that Sugar's neck.

"She ran off because you were scared," Nat said. "Horses pick up on stuff like that."

"But I *wasn't* scared until she jumped out of the ring and went tearing off like a maniac."

"You were so. Hanging on to her mouth with a death grip."

"I was not!"

Nat sniffed. "I saw what I saw. Sensitive mare like that. No wonder she tried to get rid of you."

"Okay, Nat, that'll do," Sasha broke in. "Marcy did the best she could."

"Well, she wouldn't have run away with me."

"Pooh," Marcy said, "I'll bet some horse has run away with you some time."

Nat folded her arms and looked smug. "Never."

"And what about Vince?" Sasha asked. "Remember that time we went out with the Chesterland hounds? What do you call that?"

"That was out hunting. That was different."

"I'll tell you something, Marcy," Sasha said. "If you ever have a horse running off with you again, you should turn him. Horses can think of only one thing at a time. So if you get them to think about turning, they'll forget about running."

"But how can you turn a horse when you're hanging on for dear life?"

"Same thing happens to you as happens to the

horse. If you think about turning, you won't be so worried about just hanging on. Then you'll be in control of the situation instead of letting it control you."

Marcy hoped fervently that she would never have the occasion to put this idea to the test.

Jim looked at Sasha admiringly. "I've learned more about horses in the last five minutes than in the rest of my life put together."

"It's elementary, really," Sasha said. "Horse psychology isn't very different from people psychology."

"How'd you get involved with horses?"

Sasha shrugged. "It's in my blood, I guess. You know horse people are a breed apart. Probably we were horses in a past life, or maybe we were just born in the wrong century. All I know is that the first time I saw a pony, that was it. I had to have one, and for years I was obsessed. I'm not obsessed any more, but I still love it."

"So you still ride?"

"No. A time came when I'd had enough, in fact, I thought that phase of my life was over. Time to move on. And for quite a few years I didn't have horses, or anything to do with them. I was working hard and Nat was little. Then I got a yen for the country, and Nat wanted to exchange her rocking horse for a real one, so we moved out of the city to New Jersey. Helping Nat I acquired a new passion. Teaching. There's nothing like transmitting the skills that you have, seeing your pupil work until she gets it right, watching her move from struggle to mastery, seeing her face light up when she finally gets it. I taught pony club, then started helping some of the kids at the shows. Finally it got to be too time-consuming, though. The way it is now with Nat and Marcy is just right. They're at different levels, which is interesting for me. They do all the barn work, and I just get to enjoy it."

"Teachers can be really important," Jim said. "Hearing you makes me want to try it."

"It's more satisfying to me than doing it myself, really. It's also true that sculpting is a lonely business. This horse connection keeps me active, gets me outdoors and in touch with people. It's a good balance."

"Now I'm beginning to understand why Marcy is so enthusiastic about it," Jim said.

Marcy smiled to herself when he said that. Then she noticed him looking at Sasha intently like people did in the movies when they were about to kiss each other. Sasha was looking at Jim too, with a kind of half-smile that made Marcy feel uncomfortable.

They walked on toward the house deep in conversation. Marcy trailed behind trying not to think about Sugar. She just wanted to go home and forget it.

Jim invited them in for coffee and Marcy was going to say no thank you, they ought to be getting along home, but Sasha said yes before Marcy could open her mouth. Inside, Jim and Sasha kept talking, not about anything very important—some mutual friend they had in New York and how they liked living in California and some new kind of grass mix Jim was trying in the north pasture—but they *sounded* as if it were really important and as if Marcy and Nat had ceased to exist.

Marcy slouched on the couch with a magazine, looking at them every now and then and swearing under her breath—not the made-up words she used out loud with her mother, but real ones she'd learned from T.C. She didn't think it was fair for Jim to be acting like that. Usually he was interested in *her* and made her a special drink with cherry juice and soda water. He'd tell her jokes and listen to her too. But today he offered them canned soft drinks and went on talking to Sasha. Nat sat in the corner of the room opposite Marcy tapping her foot. She didn't look too happy either. Then when Jim asked Sasha if she'd like him to show her around the ranch, Marcy and Nat forgot they were supposed to be mad at each other and banded together to get Sasha out of there.

On the way home no one said much. Sasha's mind seemed to be somewhere else, and Marcy remembered that she *was* mad at Nat. She didn't see why she had to rub it in about being a better rider and knowing more about horses than Marcy did. How could she be as good as Nat? She'd only been riding for a few months and Nat had been riding for years.

Now Marcy was back to square one. Nobody to ride but Joey, and what if Nat decided that she couldn't ride him anymore? Marcy spent the rest of the way home thinking of ways to mollify Nat, to ensure that she would be able to ride Joey. If she didn't have a horse of her own she *had* to be able to ride Joey.

Chapter 10

THE LIGHTS WERE on on the front porch and inside the house too, but even before she opened the front door Marcy knew her parents weren't home. An empty house feels like an empty house, even from the outside. Marcy slammed the front door shut, harder than she would have if her parents had been home, and waited for her mother to call, "Marcy? How many times do I have to tell you not to slam the door?" But she didn't. There weren't any reverberations from the door slamming, either. Just silence.

Marcy walked back to the kitchen, her footsteps unnaturally loud in the empty house. On the kitchen table her mother had left a note: "We're off to the opera with the Appelbaums. Hope the horse was a huge success. Lasagna and/or chicken pot pie in the freezer. Turn the oven to 350°, cook for 45 min. See you in the morning. XXX Mom." Marcy made a face, her special mad face. Huge success, sure! She was hungry, but she didn't want anything frozen. She wanted something warm, like a human being. Someone who would listen and be sympathetic while she reeled off the saga of Sugar and Kathy. Nat being supercilious. Jim and Sasha absorbed with each other, not paying any attention to her or Nat.

She took a handful of cookies from the cookie jar and went up to her room. She pulled up her jeans to look at the bruise on her calf where the stirrup had banged against it. It was turning purple already, and it hurt.

What a horrible day! The beautiful golden mare danced before her and was replaced by that tidducky Sugar. *Her* horse would never do anything like that. Her horse would whicker at her when she came to feed him in the morning, he'd snuffle her hair with his lips, and he'd never, never run away. Her horse . . . Marcy shook her head. There she was, dreaming again. Meanwhile she had a real problem: Nat.

She started pacing. She'd managed to cover most of the flowered wallpaper on the walls of her room with pictures of horses and other things: her recital program from last year, her Red Cross swimming certificates, a photograph of her and Dana at Dana's last recital, a poster of two kittens playing with a ball of yarn. She stopped in front of a story that she had found in one of Sasha's books:

> *A long time ago in China there were two friends, one who played the harp skillfully and one who listened skillfully.*
>
> *When the one played or sang about a mountain, the other would say: "I can see the mountain before us."*
>
> *When the one played about water, the listener would exclaim: "Here is the running stream!"*
>
> *But the listener fell sick and died. The first friend cut the strings of his harp and never played again. Since that time, the cutting of harp strings has always been a sign of intimate friendship.*

The story was called "True Friends," and when Marcy had first seen it, she'd copied it out and put it up on the wall, because, she thought, that's what she and Nat were. They'd made little harps out of sticks they found in the woods, strung them with fishline and then cut the strings. Then they gave each other the harps they had made. Right now the one Nat had made and given to her was hanging on the wall next to the story. Marcy ran her fingers along the curved neck of the harp and read the story again.

Some true friend she turned out to be, she thought. I wouldn't make fun of her. If she were playing about the water, then that's what I would see. Why can't she do the same? Marcy stood reading the story, then just staring at it until the words blurred and dissolved into patterns. Then she heard her father's voice in her head: "Being close with someone means accepting all of them, even the parts you don't like or wouldn't choose." Well, she wouldn't choose some parts of Nat, but she was a lot better than Susan Appelbaum, that was for sure.

At school Susan and Virginia and some of the boys they hung around with had taken to whinnying and laughing when she and Nat came into the room. Being laughed at was awful, and every time they did it Marcy shook with anger. They were stupid, though. They didn't know what it was like to canter around the ring on Joey, feel him bounding along, strong and smooth, and then have him stop on a dime, just because she pinched in with her seat and closed her fingers on the reins. Sometimes she could even get him to halt without using the reins at all. In fact, they were so stupid that, even if they did know what it was like, they wouldn't appreciate it. All of a sudden Marcy felt achy inside, and she wished that Nat was there. They could design jump courses or make up some more swear words. It was no fun being by herself.

She turned out the lights in her room and went to the window: It was time for her evening wish. She stuck her head out the window looking for a star. The one she saw first turned out to be the wing light on an airplane. She waited. When her eyes adjusted to the dark, she saw a real star and kept her eyes on it while she said:

Star light, star bright
First star I see tonight
Wish I may, wish I might
Have this wish I wish tonight.

Then she closed her eyes to make a wish. Suddenly she didn't know what to wish. She could wish for a horse, but that was old; she wished for a horse all the time. She'd even been praying for a horse. Maybe she was wearing it out. She'd wish for something else for a change—that she and Nat were friends again, that Nat wouldn't make sarcastic comments when she made a mistake riding and would let her ride Joey every day as long as she wanted to, that she didn't have to play in the audition. It was coming up on Wednesday, and she was dreading it.

She pulled her head back inside and shut the window, shivering from the cold. In spite of herself, she had to laugh. In a few minutes time she'd gone from not being able to think of even one wish to thinking of— how many was it? Three? Four? She wanted them all to come true, but in the rhyme it said "this wish," not "these wishes." She would have to choose one.

She started pacing around her room again, unable to decide. Finally she sat down and made slips of paper, numbered for each wish. Then she did "eenie, meenie, minie, mo" on the slips of paper. "This very one" turned out to be not playing in the audition. "Good," Marcy said to herself with a smile. "Good!"

* * *

ALL DAY WEDNESDAY Marcy kept thinking about
the wish, because she was running out of time. The
audition was that afternoon. Her mother had written
a note excusing her from P.E. and Math, which
ordinarily would have pleased her, but she would rather
sit through math class than play in the audition. A *lot*
rather.

Her mother picked her up at school and brought
her home to change her clothes. Then they picked up
Gene and headed across the Golden Gate Bridge to San
Francisco.

Marcy sat in the back seat not listening to her
mother and Gene in the front. She looked at the music
beside her on the seat and willed it to go away. Too late,
she thought if she'd left it at home, that would have
made her wish come true, because she couldn't play if
she didn't have any music.

When they arrived at the auditorium a few other
young players were gathered with their mothers and
teachers. Nobody except Marcy had on a plaid dress with
ruffles. If she were the judge she would flunk herself out
of the audition for wearing such a thing, but it was her
mother's idea.

She was scheduled to play at three thirty, but they
were running late. It was nearly four o'clock when her
name was called. Marcy walked up to the stage with
Gene, who was going to turn the pages for her, put her
music on the piano and began to play. In that instant
she knew what to do. She messed up the tempos, hit
wrong notes, did everything she could think of to insure

that she would not be picked to play in the next round of auditions.

When she was finished, she and Gene went and sat down with her mother again. She didn't say much, but Marcy figured she would hear about it later.

She did. On the way home her mother said, "What on earth happened to you? I've never heard you play so badly."

"I don't know, Mom." She didn't dare tell her that she'd done it on purpose, to make sure that she wouldn't have to play in any more auditions, let alone be selected to play in the performance. "I was so nervous I couldn't do anything right."

Gene gave her a sympathetic look and said, "Well, that's all part of it. If you want to be a pianist, you'll have to learn to live with nerves. It's too bad, though, because I thought you had a good chance to be chosen for the next round. Oh well," he finished, "you can chalk this one up to experience. Next time you won't be so nervous."

Next time, Marcy thought, *next* time. Cripes! As for wanting to be a pianist . . . well, this didn't seem like the right time to go into *that*.

Marcy was putting her music away when the phone rang. She was getting so much satisfaction out of putting it away, thinking about how she wouldn't have to play it any more, that she let her mother answer it.

"It's for you, Marcy," she called.

"How did the audition go?" Nat asked when Marcy answered the phone.

"Uh, I'll tell you in a minute," Marcy said and went upstairs where she could talk without her mother listening. On the way upstairs she realized that she was surprised Nat had called. Ever since the day at Jim's ranch she'd been quiet and moody, and Marcy thought she was still mad at her. "What do you want to know for?"

"Was it scary? Were there lots of people there? Were you nervous? How did you do?" Nat fired the questions at her, sounding as if she was really interested. "Marce? You still there?"

"Yeah."

"Why don't you tell me? I really want to know. Get it?"

"I thought you were still mad at me."

"Oh, zurgle that. Nothing to do with you. It's . . . uh . . . something else."

"What?" Marcy went on pressing, but Nat wouldn't say any more, switched back to asking Marcy about the audition.

"You'll love it," Marcy said, finally believing that she really did want to know. Then she told her what she'd done and Nat laughed.

"You're a stitch. Gutsy."

"I guess," Marcy said, feeling more satisfied when she heard the admiration in Nat's voice. "See, I figured if I really blew it, maybe, just maybe, my mother would let me quit. Then I'd have more time to ride if—" She broke off, worried again. She'd been concentrating on

the audition and hadn't ridden since the day she tried
Sugar. "I mean, if it's okay with you."

"Well, of course it is."

"But you said Joey was getting sour."

"I said I didn't want him to *get* sour. It's been
incredibly boring these last few days while you were
glued to the piano. And you're going to have your own
horse pretty soon anyway."

"I can ride Joey until then?"

"Sure. How 'bout tomorrow? And Marce?"

"Hm?"

"I'm sorry I said that stuff to you about Sugar. I
think maybe I was feeling a little bit jealous."

"Of me? Come on."

"Sasha's always going on about how you have a
natural feel, and how good you're going to be, and—"

"Oh sure. Getting run off with."

"That mare was hot," Nat said. "Not your fault.
And . . . anyway, I'm sorry."

"It's okay," Marcy said, embarrassed. Nat jealous
of *her*?

After she hung up she realized Nat hadn't told her
what the "something else" was she had on her mind.

FOR THE NEXT few days her mother didn't say anything to her about practicing, so Marcy took advantage
of the unexpected freedom by staying over at Nat's
longer than usual. After they'd ridden, they spent a
long time cooling Joey out and grooming him. They

spent so much time brushing him that he was shiny as a silver dollar.

When it got dark they'd go into the house where they'd play Scrabble or listen to records or get started on their homework. One evening the front door bell rang and they looked at each other in surprise. No one at Nat's house ever used the front door, let along rang the bell.

Nat went to answer it with Marcy trailing behind. When she saw who it was Marcy was even more surprised. Jim Ferguson. What was he doing at Nat's house? While she was trying to figure that out she heard him ask for Sasha. And she heard Nat tell him that she wasn't home.

"But I called this afternoon," Jim said, "she said she'd be here."

Nat shrugged. "She's pretty absentminded sometimes."

"I brought some wood," Jim said. "We cut down an old cherry tree at the ranch and she said she'd like some. It's got beautiful grain." He stood in the doorway looking puzzled.

Nat seemed to realize that he was disappointed too. "She'll probably be back soon," she said. "She took some work to South San Francisco to be crated for shipping. She's probably stuck in traffic." Then she offered their services to help him unload the wood. But Marcy said she had to get on home, and she left. Behind her the lights were switched on in the garage and she could hear the deep rumble of Jim's voice and the higher tones of

Nat's and the chunking of wood as they unloaded his truck.

When Marcy got home she found that her mother had returned to normal. She was looking at her watch and tapping her foot. She told Marcy that she'd been spending too much time over at Nat's. She'd been neglecting the piano.

"But I want to neglect the piano," Marcy said. Then her mother got conveniently deaf and went on talking about how important it was to practice, as if Marcy hadn't said a word.

Marcy sat down at the piano and did exercises from Hanon until it was time for dinner. Lost in the beat of the metronome, she almost forgot about Jim over at Nat's and the companionable buzz of their voices as they worked together unloading the wood.

Chapter 11

ON THE DAY when they went to look at Sugar, Sasha had said, "Don't worry. We'll find something," and Marcy's father said, "Oh I'm sure there are lots of horses that would be fine for you," but when Sasha said the same thing after they went to look at the next horse, and the next, and the next, Marcy did begin to worry. Fall turned to winter, but still they hadn't found anything suitable, and Marcy didn't feel any nearer to having a horse of her own than she had on the day when they'd gone to look at Sugar.

"Well," Sasha said, "consider how much you've learned."

"Yeah," Marcy said, "I've learned that there's not

one horse in the whole world that's right for me. If they're pretty, they can't jump worth spit. If they're good jumpers, they're too hot or they're not sound. Or, if they're okay jumpers and pretty good looking, then they're too green or too expensive. They're always *too* something."

"We haven't been having the best of luck," Sasha agreed.

"I know. Maybe I should give up. Maybe it's not in the cards for me to have a horse."

"Quit riding?" Sasha asked, and Marcy winced.

"No. I don't want to quit riding. I just want to quit looking for a horse. I'm tired of it."

"And have one drop into your lap?"

"Uh-huh."

"Well, guess what?"

"What?"

"That's how it happens in fairy tales, but not in real life. If you want to find something, you have to look for it. Get active."

"Yes," Jim said, "your dad and I looked for a whole year before we found Three Springs Ranch."

Marcy looked at Jim and nodded. He was over at the Joneses almost all the time these days. With part of her she was getting used to it. But another part of her still felt betrayed, especially when he looked at Sasha with this particular funny look—direct and intense, soft and smoky, all at the same time. When that happened Marcy might as well have been a sofa cushion for all she was noticed. Then her insides would start moving around in a way that felt peculiar, as if the glue that held her organs in place wasn't working anymore. But that didn't happen too often, she had to admit. Most of the time she enjoyed seeing him more often than she had in the past. He still listened to her the way he used to and told funny stories and was thoughtful and quiet. For a grown-up he was pretty good company.

"I fell into something close to despair," Jim continued. "I was even going to make an offer on a shabby piece of land out near Bodega Bay. Fortunately, your father talked me out of it. He was sure we would find something better."

"I guess I'm a person of little faith," Marcy said. "*I'm* not sure."

"Well, I am," Sasha said. "Just have patience. And keep looking. It's not the time to give up, but to press on."

"Okay," Marcy said, not fully convinced, "but I'm not feeling patient. I was hoping to have a horse by now. I want to go to that show in January in Santa Rosa."

"You might have to pass that one up. But even if you don't have your own horse by then, you could come and groom for Nat. You can learn a lot by watching."

After the show she'd been to with Nat, Marcy didn't want to go to any more shows as a spectator or as a groom. Hanging on the rail, watching other people go into the ring, she was seized with a powerful desire to be in the ring too. She might learn something by watching, but she'd learn a lot more by doing it. "Couldn't I ride Joey too? At least in the flat classes?"

Sasha shook her head. "You're in the same age group. If you rode Joey, then who would Nat ride?"

Marcy couldn't think of an answer to that. She needed her own horse, all right.

IN DECEMBER IT started to rain. It rained and rained and rained, as if trying to make up for all the months of drought. It wasn't even much fun at the barn, slogging around in the mud with rain drizzling down her neck.

Christmas came and went. It was the best Christmas Marcy had ever had, and the worst. The worst, because Dana didn't come home and Marcy was all by herself; the best, because she got a saddle, the only thing, besides a horse, that she truly wanted.

On Christmas night she went to bed with her saddle beside her. The new leather smelled delicious, and Marcy thought dreamily of the day when she could put it on her own horse. But when she closed her eyes she saw her stocking hanging all by itself on the mantelpiece looking lonely, as if it knew that Dana's stocking should have been hanging beside it. Dana had a part in *The Nutcracker*, and Marcy knew it was a great opportunity for her, but she thought coming home for the vacation was more important than dancing in *The Nutcracker*. They could have had a Christmas cookie decorating contest like they always did and gone carolling with the choir. Always before they'd decorated the tree together on Christmas Eve and awakened each other early on Christmas morning, giggling, hovering around in the upstairs hall, giddy with anticipation while they waited for their parents to get up. Marcy, being younger, went down the stairs first, and Dana was always right behind her . . .

Dana danced into her room in the pink tutu of the Sugar Plum Fairy. A tiara sparkled in her hair as she danced across the stage awash in rosy light, making lovely floating leaps and perfect dervish turns that left the audience gasping. Marcy looked closer and saw that the stage had given way to something else. It was the same color as the stage, but softer, and slightly rounded —it was her saddle! Dana didn't notice, danced on.

"Hey, that's my saddle," Marcy called from the audience, but her voice was lost in the swell of the music. Dana finished the dance, curtsied, blew kisses to the people in the audience, who were clapping and cheering. Her mother appeared from stage left carrying a huge bouquet of roses. She swept across the stage, placing her feet toe first, like a dancer, stopped beside Dana and, with a sweeping curtsey, presented the roses to her. The audience went wild, clapping and yelling, "Brava! Bravissima!" and the sound of the clapping went on and on . . .

When Marcy opened her eyes she mumbled, "That wasn't clapping, just rain on the roof." And it certainly was raining, in a steady downpour that drummed on the roof with a din. "She wasn't the Sugar Plum Fairy either," Marcy went on, "no tutu, no tiara, no roses. She was just a mouse in that fight between the Nutcracker and the Mouse King."

She worked on her saddle with saddle soap and

neat's-foot oil to soften the new leather, but couldn't get the image of Dana out of her mind. Her mother and Dana on stage, smiling at the audience, smiling at each other. When she got a horse, it wouldn't be like that: She would be the one on the saddle, not doing something silly like dancing on it, but sitting in it the way one was supposed to and dressed properly in breeches and boots. When she entered the ring all heads would turn, and in the end, she would have a blue ribbon . . . and . . . and . . . a bouquet of roses? Marcy shook her head. Somehow that didn't quite fit, and her horse might eat the roses.

ONE SUNDAY TOWARD the end of January she got up early so she would have time to read the ads in the paper before church. She came down the stairs and stared at the rain pouring down outside. Enough is enough, Marcy thought, as she grabbed a poncho off the coatrack and ran out to get the paper. It's great that the drought is over, but if this keeps up we better start building an ark.

The paper was wrapped in plastic, but still it was wet. In the kitchen she put the front and back sections in the oven to dry, but the Want Ads Section was in the middle and was only damp around the edges. In the Horses-Stock column there were Holstein heifers advertised, pigs, silver pheasants and fancy bantams, "horse trailers for less," and, actually, some horses. She circled three to call when she got home from church.

In church she kept seeing the ads in the paper. Even

when she was on her knees, the newsprint swam up in front of her and dissolved into a bright bay mare galloping across a field. Marcy watched her mane wisping in the wind and heard hardly any of the church service.

By the time she got home the rain had slowed to a drizzle. Marcy changed into Levi's, grabbed the paper and ran over to Nat's. The back door was locked, which was unusual. Marcy ran around to the front and saw that the truck was gone. She looked blankly at the space where the truck was usually parked, wondering where they had gone. Sunday mornings they were always home.

Puzzled, she went out to the barn to wait, hoping they'd be back soon. Some of the ads in the paper looked promising and unless she called soon someone else might get there first. She said hi to Joey, then stopped and looked into the empty stall next to his, the one she and Nat had designated for her horse. "Listen here, stall," she said, "you won't be empty much longer. Pretty soon you're going to have my horse to keep you company. Maybe even today." Then she went into the ring and started cantering absently about. She was practicing doing flying changes, which was difficult, because she only had two legs. If she had four legs like a horse she would be able to do it properly, with that slight little hesitation that always made her catch her breath.

She was executing a half-turn in reverse when she heard the truck pull into the driveway. She cantered out the gate, around the corner of the house, and saw that it wasn't Sasha's gray truck, or Jim's either, but T.C.'s.

"Hi, T.C.!"

"Ho, there, Marcy."

"I thought this was Sunday. You don't work on Sundays, do you?"

"Not usually, but I need to put another coat of sealer on that counter. I thought I would be able to do it yesterday, but with this damp weather the first coat wasn't dry enough."

"Want some help?"

"Well, sure, punkin, I wouldn't say no to an extra pair of hands."

Marcy stood behind T.C. while he unlocked the door to Sasha's studio. Inside it smelled of fresh wood and turpentine. It was a big, open room with a high, beamed ceiling and walls of weathered gray wood from the old shed. One end, for designing and thinking, had a long countertop and a bank of windows. The other was for working and would contain all the machines and tools Sasha used for making her sculptures.

"I'd love to have a place like this," Marcy said. "Just being here makes me feel quiet and peaceful. It would be a wonderful place to work, or just to sit and think."

"Well, I reckon. Settin' and thinkin' ain't exactly my line. Now you take this here can and do that counter-top startin' from the end."

After they had been working for a while, T.C. laid his brush down and hunkered down to roll a cigarette. "You're awful quiet today," he said.

Marcy set down her brush and looked at T.C. Behind him was a mosaic of windows, some beveled glass, some stained glass, some plain. Depending on which window you looked through, the trees outside changed shape and color. "I wanted to talk to Nat and Sasha about the horses advertised in the paper, but they're not here. I keep seeing horses everywhere. I bet you didn't know there was a little roan mare there, did you?" she asked, pointing to the beveled glass window just behind T.C. "See her running through the trees?"

"Wal, now, honey, there ain't no horse in them treetops."

"Oh, I know, but I see her just the same. I was even seeing horses this morning in church."

T.C. whistled. "Sounds like you better do something about that."

Marcy sighed. "I know. I'm trying to. But I need advice about these horses," she said, tapping the paper.

"Let's see," T.C. said. "Maybe I can help."

Marcy took the paper over to him. "See the ones I've marked? Those are the ones I thought might do for me."

T.C. took the paper and held it out at arm's length the way farsighted people do when they're trying to read without their glasses. He read the first one Marcy had circled: " 'T.B. 3 yrs. Filly 16 hnds. Show ribbn. winr. Jumper trng. Sound. Gentle.' Well, now. Might be okay for Nat, but you don't want no three-year-old. Green horses and green riders is like water and oil. They don't mix. One of you ought to know what you're doin'. And since you don't, you ought to have a horse that does."

"I know. That's what Sasha says too, but everything else sounds so good! I can just see her, jet black with the look of eagles. She would have a snow white bridle and saddle that would glisten like the moon. I would call her Midnight Maid—"

"Now, honey, that sounds like one of your treetop horses. Let's see about a real one: '15.2 geld. experienced rider only.' Whoa now. You know what that means?"

Marcy shook her head.

"It means that whoever owns this horse can't ride 'em. Probably God himself couldn't. I wouldn't touch that one with a ten-foot pole.

"Okay, let's see—'Pony hunter. 14.2 9 yr. mare. Honest jumper.' You don't want a pony do you?"

"Not really, but I'm getting desperate. And it says she's an honest jumper."

"Yeah. What it don't say is that she runs away, or bites your rear when you're trying to get on. Ponies are smart, generally a lot smarter than the kids who ride them. And it don't take them very long to figure that out and come up with a whole barrelful of tricks."

"Phooey," Marcy said, "those are the only horses that look likely this week. By the time I find a horse I'll be too old and creaky to ride it."

"Now, now. Give yourself at least another year before you're put out to pasture for good."

"Oh, all right." She laughed. "I guess it's not that bad, huh?"

"I can think of lots of worse things." T.C. lapsed

into silence and blew smoke rings into the air. Try as she might to snare them with her finger, they dissolved into wisps before her approaching hand.

"Well, I reckon I ought to get back to work," T.C. said, stubbing out his cigarette. "That counter ain't gettin' sealed while we're settin' here chewin' the fat." He pulled the beak of his cap down over his forehead and went to pick up his brush. He dipped it into the can of sealer and was about to take a stroke when he put it down and snapped his fingers. "Blowed if I didn't almost fergit!"

"Forget what?"

"About Hoyt. You 'member me tellin' you about my old buddy, Hoyt?"

Marcy shook her head.

"The one that's the blacksmith? That I knew back in Oklahoma?"

Marcy shook her head again.

"Well, him and me used to pal around together when we was young bucks on the rodeo circuit. We were a great calf ropin' team and we had some good times, old Hoyt and me . . ." T.C. trailed off, raised and lowered his cap. ". . . and then what with one thing and another we lost track of each other for a pretty good spell. Then a couple of years ago—" He stopped again. "Goddamn if it wasn't closer to ten—time sure gets away from you when you're as old and creaky as me— I run into him out at the Safeway. Imagine that! I-ma-gine," he repeated, drawing out each syllable, "and I tell you it was like old home week. We hightailed it

from that piddlin' plastic excuse for a grocery store—
why, do you know what a real grocery store is? No, don't
reckon you would—over to Smoky Joe's and ordered us
up a couple of beers and . . ." He took off his hat and
scratched his head. "What was we talkin' about?"

"Horses," Marcy said, "the ones in the paper."

"That's right. That's right. Now it's comin' back to
me. Long way 'round Robin Hood's barn, but I'm gettin'
there. The point is that he's took up horseshoein' now.
I saw him just the other day and he said there was a nice
little horse out at Foggy Creek Stables that was abandoned, near as he could tell."

"Abandoned? How could anyone abandon a horse?
I sure wouldn't do that."

"I know you wouldn't. But there's all sorts of people in this world and some of 'em ain't very nice. Think
a horse is like a automobile. Just take it out, stuff it with
gas and cram your foot down on the accelerator—whenever it suits you. And if it don't, just leave 'em settin' in
a stall gettin' obese or foundered or worse. Horses ain't
cars. You can't treat 'em like that. Why, did I ever tell
you about Mary McCrary? She was a—"

"T.C.," Marcy said. She knew it wasn't polite to
interrupt, but she was on the track of a horse, and if
T.C. got launched into a story it might be hours before
she could get him back to the point. "The horse," she
prompted, "that Hoyt saw. Out at Foggy Creek."

"Oh, yeah. Well, Hoyt says he's been shoein' that
horse for free for almost six months now. Leastways
might as well be, because he keeps sendin' the bills, but

nobody's payin' 'em. So when he was out there last week he went in to see the manager, Ben Carlson, to find out what the deal was. Carlson said they owed six months board on him too. The girl that owned him had moved to Hawaii and told him she was gonna send for the horse, but it's been six months and he hasn't heard from her. Not one peep. He tried writin' her in Hawaii, but he got his letter back with 'No Such' written on it, so as far as he's concerned, it's his horse now. 'Cept he don't want it."

"So what's going to happen to the horse?"

"Well, now, that's the point. It occurred to me that he might be just the horse for you. Hoyt said he was a pretty nice horse, and Hoyt knows a pretty nice horse when he sees one, I'll tell you that."

Marcy's whole self got very still and quiet, and a strange roaring noise sounded in her ears. "Do you think we could go look at him?" she whispered.

"Right now?"

"No time like the present. I've heard you say that, haven't I?"

"Yep. Well, okay. Let's finish this here countertop, then I reckon we could go."

Chapter 12

AS THEY PULLED into the stable T.C. said, "Now don't go expectin' too much in the looks department. A horse that's been neglected for six months is going to look scraggly-assed."

"I know," Marcy said.

T.C. whistled. "This sure is a fancy place."

Marcy looked at the neat white fences, the flowerboxes bordering the driveway and the large airy barn with a cupola on top. She had to agree with T.C. Inside the barn, on the right, was a room marked "Office."

While T.C. was in the office talking to Mr. Carlson, Marcy walked through the barn. The aisle was swept clean and each horse's halter hung on a brass hook by the side of his stall. On the front of each stall was a name plate with the horse's name on it, and underneath, that of the owner. There was also a card with the horse's feeding schedule on it, in English and Spanish, and the name of his vet. The horses all looked shiny and healthy, and they snuffled curiously when Marcy came up to their stalls.

When T.C. came out of the office, they set off down the drive, away from the big barn, following Mr. Carlson's directions. They turned left behind the covered ring at the end of the drive and saw a row of paddocks. They were made of wood that had once been painted white, but was now peeling and flaking and pocked with irregular half-moons chewed out along the top. Half of each paddock was covered with a metal roof. The horses here didn't look as clean or as fat as the ones in the barn. Two of them were fighting with each other over the fence and had scars along their necks.

"Just about every place and every body has its backside," T.C. said. "Let's see now. He said he was in the tenth one from the end. Is this the tenth one?"

Marcy counted and nodded. She walked eagerly up to the paddock.

"I told you not to expect too much," T.C. said.

"Oh, he's not so bad," Marcy said. "I like bays and isn't that a cute blaze?" The horse had a narrow white stripe that ran down his face and tailed off to the left between his nostrils.

"That's called a stripe. A blaze is wider." T.C. stood off looking at the horse with narrowed, critical eyes. It was the same look Sasha had when she was sizing up a horse.

"I can't tell nothin' about his legs when he's standin' in that muck," T.C. said. "Whyn't you grab his halter and we'll stand him up out there on the road."

Marcy looked around for his halter, but she couldn't find it.

T.C. clucked. "That's dangerous. If there was a fire that poor horse would fry while someone was tryin' to locate a halter. Well, just go down the row and grab one from some other paddock. We'll put it back when we're done."

Marcy got a halter and led the horse out onto the road and stood him up while T.C. walked around looking at him, feeling his legs, looking at his feet and his teeth. Then he had her lead him up and down at a walk and a trot.

Finally he said, "Well, Hoyt was right. That's a pretty nice horse, all right. What do you think of him, punkin?"

"Well," Marcy said. "He's dirty, and he's kind of thin, but I can feed him and clean him up. Then he'll look a lot better. I like the way he's put together and the way he stands, as if he were proud of himself. And he's so friendly."

T.C. smiled at her. "You're learnin', all right. Fat looks good, and a shiny coat—but those things are just window dressing. This horse ain't in very good shape, but he's sure put together right. Seems to have a real good disposition too. You want to try him?"

"I sure do."

"You didn't think about bringin' no tack did you?"

"Yes, I did," Marcy said, pleased that her disappointing ventures up to now had taught her something useful. "I put my saddle and Joey's bridle in your truck while you were cleaning up."

There was a small ring in the trees behind the paddocks and they decided to try the horse there, in private, rather than go into the big front ring where other people were riding. The horse stood quietly while they tacked him up, and Marcy got on. He was a little looky going down to the ring, but he walked quietly enough and didn't spook at anything. After Marcy walked, trotted and cantered him both directions of the ring, she pulled up and came over to T.C., who was standing in the middle.

"What do you think now?" he asked.

"He's wonderful," Marcy said, throwing her arms around his neck. "His gaits are really smooth, and he has a nice mouth. He doesn't feel as powerful as Joey, but he's not lazy either; he moves right out when I squeeze with my legs."

"He looks real good to me. 'Course he'll feel more powerful when he's had steady work and gets muscled up. But he's a real nice mover. Real nice. Whyn't you pop him over this little crossrail and see if he can jump?"

Marcy's heart was slamming against the wall of her chest. She had never jumped except when Sasha was there to tell her exactly what to do. She took a deep breath and trotted up to the crossrail, trying to remember everything Sasha had told her. Almost before she knew it, he was over the jump and cantering away from it. She did that a few more times, trotting in and cantering off, feeling pleased with herself. The horse felt confident and eager under her as if he enjoyed it too. T.C. made the crossrail into a little vertical and she trotted that a few times. Then she cantered it, and let out a Rebel yell—"eeeeehah!"—that she'd learned from T.C. This horse was so much fun!

"Okay, sweetie, that's enough." T.C. said. "Walk him around until he's cooled off. Then we'll go up and have a talk with that 'ere Carlson."

Marcy walked and walked. She kept walking long after the horse was cool. It felt so good to be on him that she never wanted to land on the ground again. But T.C. said it was getting late, so she put him back into his paddock and hung the halter back on the nail where she'd gotten it. "Bye, bye, sweet horse," she said. "My horse," she added, almost under her breath.

"Don't go countin' your chickens before they're hatched," T.C. said.

The horse whickered at Marcy as she started off down the drive, and when she looked back he was standing in the corner of his paddock nearest her, with his ears pricked toward her. The stripe curling over his nose made him look as if he were smiling at her.

Marcy's heart leaped. "Richard," she said. "I just know he wants to be mine."

"Huh?"

"His name is Richard—after Richard the Lion-hearted. He's my favorite king of England—so bold and dashing and courageous. That's exactly what he's like," Marcy concluded, nodding her head with satisfaction.

"He's a good 'un, all right," T.C. said, but he sounded as if he were thinking about something else.

When they were partway up the drive on their way back to the big barn he stopped and rolled a cigarette. "You let me do the talkin'." he said. "And try not to appear eager. I've locked horns with some pretty ornery horse traders in my day, and I don't like the look of this Carlson. Shifty-eyed son of a bitch. He said we could have him for the price of the board. Let's see, board's a hundred fifty a month. Can you imagine one fifty a month for that tiddly-ass little corral that ain't even clean and that's freezing and wet in the winter and hotter'n blue blazes in the summer? That's highway robbery. So what does that come out to?"

"Nine hundred dollars," Marcy said.

"That too much for you?"

Marcy shook her head. "That Appaloosa we looked at last week was more than twice that and Daddy said it was okay."

"Just between you, me and the gatepost, that's a bargain for a horse like that. But don't let on to Carlson that we know that. We'll just act real dumb and talk about how poor he looks."

"Okay," Marcy said.

When they went into the office she could see why T.C. had called Mr. Carlson shifty-eyed. He had strange no-color eyes that slid all over the place, but never looked right at you.

"This here's Marcy," T.C. said, "the one that wants to buy that little bay horse down in the paddocks."

"How do you do?" he said, holding out his hand.

Marcy shook. His hand felt limp and clammy as a three-day-old fish.

T.C. readjusted his cap. "We took a look at that horse," he said, "and he don't look none too good."

"Yes?" Mr. Carlson said and opened his mouth again, as if he were about to go on. But he didn't. He shut it and waited for T.C.

"He's all right," T.C. said in his flattest voice, "but he ain't in very good shape. Can't say as how he's had an oversupply of groceries."

"All of our horses are fed two flakes of excellent quality oat hay in the morning, alfalfa in the evening, and a mixed grain ration at noon."

"If that horse has been eatin' that much just settin' around, he must have a heap of worms in his belly."

"All of our horses are on a regular worming program," Mr. Carlson said turning to the filing cabinet behind his desk. "Here's the card on that horse. He was last wormed a little over two months ago."

T.C. peered at the card. "Well, I can see that it *says* that. Could have fooled me."

Mr. Carlson's lip curled slightly.

T.C. appeared not to notice, but his voice got even flatter. Marcy had never seen him get mad before, but she had the feeling that she was about to.

"Well now," he said, "I reckon Marcy here might like to take that horse off your hands. Seems like he might be okay for a kid's horse. To putter around on the trails and stuff. You said she could have him for the price of the board bill, ain't that right?"

"Yes," said Mr. Carlson, looking at the card again, "for the amount of the board bill, plus my other out-of-pocket expenses. The board for the last six months amounts to nine hundred dollars. Then there's the bill from Dr. Vlasik, the vet. That's one hundred. And the farrier is ninety. That's a total of one thousand ninety dollars."

"I don't recollect you saying nothin' about any vet bills. You said the board bill would settle it. And seein' as how he's in such bad shape, we'll make you an offer of seven hundred dollars," T.C. said.

"The price is one thousand ninety."

"Eight hundred," T.C. said.

Mr. Carlson started to get up from his chair. "If you'll excuse me, I'm a busy man."

"Oh please, Mr. Carlson," Marcy cried, fighting back the tears, "I've been looking and looking, and I love this horse. Please?"

Carlson settled back into his chair and slid his eyes over in the general direction of where Marcy was sitting. "I'm sorry, little girl, but I'm not in this for my health.

I'll not be making a penny on that horse if I sell him for one thousand ninety."

"Now look here, Carlson," T.C. broke in, "I may not be wearing no slick red pants or be settin' around in a fancy office, but horse flesh I do know, and you'd be lucky to get eight hundred for a bag of bones like that. He's not gonna look any better, either, unless someone starts takin' care of him. He's just goin' to be settin' around here, eatin' and takin' up space that might be occupied by a payin' customer. That ain't goin' to help your finances, is it?"

For the first time Mr. Carlson looked uneasy. "You may know something about horses, but business is business, and I can't afford to lose any money on that horse."

"You won't be losin' any money. In fact, you'll wish you'd given him to me by the time I'm through. There's a thing or two goin' on around here that maybe your other boarders would like to know about. And the Better Business Bureau. And maybe the SPCA would like to see the condition of the horses in them back paddocks, not to mention what Vlasik and Hoyt might like to hear. You wouldn't be makin' a hell of a lot of money if you was shut down, now, would you? And had a coupla lawsuits to boot?"

Carlson's eyes rested briefly on T.C.'s, then they started flicking around the room again. He picked up the card from his desk and turned it back and forth in his fingers. Then he smiled, with his mouth, but the no-color eyes were as expressionless as lead. "So that's the way the wind is blowing," he said at last.

"Could be," T.C. said in the same flat voice.

Carlson was silent for a while. Finally he said, "All right. You can have him for . . . nine hundred dollars. You can come and get him, but don't let me ever catch you poking around here again."

IN THE TRUCK, on the way home, T.C. said, "Didn't I tell you he was ornery? It takes a lot to get me riled, but I was gettin' riled, all right. I don't take to slick-looking oily crooks like that."

"How do you know he's a crook?"

"Because I'll bet you dollars to doughnuts that he didn't pay that vet bill any more than he paid Hoyt's. He just saw a chance to grab a little extra money for himself."

"But that's crooked!"

"Sure, it's crooked. Fella like that don't know what honest is. He's got a dollar sign for a heart. I'll bet you something else."

"What?"

"If he ever catches up with that little girl that owned him before he'll try to stick her for the whole kit and caboodle."

"Then he'd be making almost one thousand dollars free and clear."

T.C. nodded. "You got it. And you can bet it wouldn't be the first time either. We was lucky we had a little inside information like we did from Hoyt, or he might have bamboozled us."

"He did have me bamboozled. I believed him. But you're a good fighter, T.C. Thanks."

"My pleasure," T.C. said. "Horse tradin'! Shoot. I wasn't born yesterday."

"I guess not," Marcy said. "Oh, I can't wait to tell Mom and Dad, and Sasha and Nat and . . . and Jim. This is the happiest day of my life!" she said, bouncing up and down on the seat with excitement.

T.C. beamed at her and winked, settled his cap on his head and put the truck into gear.

When T.C. let her off at her house, Marcy ran up the front walk. "Mom! Dad!" she yelled, "guess what?"

"What?" her mother called from the kitchen.

"I did it! I did it!"

"Did what?"

"Found a horse!"

"How wonderful! Was it one of the ones in the paper?"

"No, it was one that Hoyt—he's a friend of T.C.'s —knew about out at Foggy Creek Stables. Oh, I'm so happy! I thought it would never happen!"

"Is it a nice horse?"

"Nice? He's not *nice*; he's perfect! Bay with a little stripe and one white sock, and he has wonderful gaits and the disposition of a lamb and jumps like a dream."

"What's all this racket?" asked her father, coming into the kitchen. Marcy turned and grabbed him, pulled him around in a little jig. "I found a horse, Daddy, I found a horse!" she sang over and over.

"Well, that's terrific, Marshmallow."

"Oh, just wait 'til you see him. He's gorgeous! And he's lucky."

"How so?"

"He has one white sock."

"So?"

" 'One white foot, buy a horse,

    Two white feet, try a horse,

    Three white feet, look well about him,

Four white feet, do without him.' " Marcy chanted. "So what do you think of that?"

Her father raised his eyebrows. "Maybe an old wives' tale?"

"No, Daddy, it's *true*."

Chapter 13

MARCY WANTED TO go get her horse on the very day she saw him, but one thing and another kept intervening. First Sasha said she wanted to see him go before Marcy put her cash on the barrelhead. So, on Tuesday, Marcy went out to Foggy Creek again, this time with Sasha and Nat. After she'd seen Richard go, Sasha said that Marcy and T.C. ought to set up a dealer barn. Marcy thought she was joking about that, but she knew that Sasha liked Richard a lot—she said he was by far the nicest horse they'd seen, and the price was reasonable too.

"See," she said, "you didn't give up. Patience pays off—and exploring all your options."

"So let's take him home," Marcy said. "I don't want him to spend one more minute in that mucky old paddock."

But Sasha said that he ought to be checked out by the vet, Dr. Vlasik, to make sure he was sound. Dr. Vlasik looked at him on Wednesday and Richard passed the physical exam with flying colors, but Dr. Vlasik also took X rays of his legs and feet to make sure there were no changes in the bones that would cause trouble later on, and the X rays took a day to develop. Marcy jittered all the way through Thursday waiting to hear. When Dr. Vlasik called on Thursday evening and said the X rays looked good Marcy felt the rush of excitement she'd had on Sunday all over again. This was it! A horse of her own at last!

Friday was gray and cold. At school Marcy kept looking out the window and hoping it wouldn't rain. This was the most important day of her life, and she thought the sun ought to shine on it. But she couldn't order up the weather and *it* didn't seem to care that that afternoon she was going to get her horse. Her very own. At last.

When school was over she and Nat climbed into the truck with Sasha, and low scudding gray clouds followed them all the way out to Foggy Creek Stables. Rain fell in intermittent spatters and the wind swirled wet leaves in the gutters. When they arrived at the barn Marcy gave a check to Mr. Carlson and ran down to the paddocks swinging her new red nylon halter. They loaded her horse in the trailer, shut up the back, and they were off.

Marcy sat beside Nat next to the window with the fingers on both hands crossed. Every now and then she glanced back to make sure her horse was all right. Through the window of the trailer she could see the white stripe on his face moving back and forth as he shifted to keep his balance.

"Be careful, okay, Sasha?" Marcy asked.

"Sure, I'm always careful when I'm hauling a horse," she said. "Why so worried?"

"I don't know. It's just that it's taken me so long to find a horse, now that I have one, I'm afraid that something will happen before we get him home. That's why I have my fingers crossed," she finished, holding up her hands.

"Well, we don't have that far to go," Sasha said, "and I've hauled lots of horses many a mile without any trouble. I'll get him there safely."

Marcy kept her fingers crossed anyway. Sasha was as good as her word and before long they pulled into the driveway, without any mishaps.

After they'd untied Richard and let down the ramp, Marcy and Nat stood to the side and watched as he backed out, placing first one hind foot on the ramp, then the other, setting them down gingerly, as he tested the quality of the footing. As soon as his head appeared Nat reached across and grabbed the lead rope.

Richard threw his head high in the air and snorted with short sharp cracks that were like no sound Marcy had ever heard coming from a horse before. He raised his tail so it waffled over his back like a fan and pranced and jigged up and down with his neck arched, wheeling around and around as if he wanted to look in all directions at once.

"What's wrong with him?" Marcy cried.

"Nothing," Nat said, "he's excited, that's all." She jerked on the lead rope and talked to him, trying to get him to relax. In a few minutes he lowered his tail and stopped prancing and snorting, but he still looked wild-eyed and tense. When they started for the barn he shied at a branch whipping in the wind. Marcy walked beside Nat wondering what on earth she'd gotten herself in for. At Foggy Creek he had been quiet and sensible, but now he seemed like a different horse altogether.

That morning, Marcy had put fresh shavings in his stall, filled up his water bucket and put a flake of hay in one corner. Now she opened the door of the stall for Nat, who led Richard inside. In a minute Nat came out and hung the halter on the hook beside the door.

"Help!" Marcy said. "I'll never be able to ride him. What am I going to do? My parents are coming over to see him and they'll think I'm crazy for sure, buying a horse that acts like a wild thing."

"He just needs to get used to it here. But I think it would be a good idea to longe him before you ride him. Let him blow off some steam."

Marcy nodded and gulped. She couldn't imagine riding him when he was acting like that.

Nat went to ride Joey while Marcy stayed by Richard's stall with her elbows propped on his door and her chin in her hands. First he sniffed every corner of his stall. He inspected the water bucket and the hay, but didn't eat or drink. He moved restlessly around, pawing in the corners, coming to the door to look out, then turning back to inspect his stall again. Then he rolled in the fresh shavings. What with the shavings, the caked-on mud and his long winter coat, he was far from looking like the glossy creatures Marcy had seen at the show. "Never mind," she said to him, "I'll get you cleaned up and you'll look just as good as the rest of them. I hope," she added dubiously, because he looked more like a furry bear who had been living in a mudhole than anything else she could think of.

By the time Nat had finished riding Joey, Richard had calmed down considerably, and when they put him in the crossties to tack him up he stood quietly enough.

While Marcy put her saddle on him and fastened the girth, Nat asked, "What kind of bit do you suppose he goes in?"

"Well, I used Joey's bridle on him before, remember?" Marcy said, "and he was fine."

"That's right," Nat said, reaching for Joey's bridle. "Sasha will be pleased. She believes in the snaffle bit. It's the simplest and the best."

When Nat had finished adjusting the bridle, Marcy took the longe line and the whip and they walked together to the ring, with Nat leading Richard. In the ring Nat looped the reins twice around his neck and snapped the longe line onto the bit ring. "Okay," she said, "walk." He stood looking at her. "Walk," she said more firmly and shook the whip at him.

Marcy could almost see him think, *Oh, this,* as he turned and walked away from Nat, circling around her. He rolled his eyes at Marcy sitting on the rail, at the jumps, at the trees blowing in the wind, but he wasn't firecracker nervous like he was when he'd first come out of the trailer, just curious.

"Trot!" Nat said.

He trotted with his ears flicking back and forth every so often to get a reading from Nat. It always amazed Marcy to see a horse being longed, controlled only by a person standing thirty feet away with a not-very-strong line in her hands. "It shows the basic good will and obedience that horses have," Sasha said, the first time Marcy had mentioned it. "They don't know their own power, thank goodness."

"Canter," Nat said, and Richard struck off into a canter. Then, just as Sasha and Marcy's parents arrived, he kicked up his heels and took off bucking and squealing.

"Is that your horse?" her mother asked.

"Yes," Marcy said, "Isn't he lovely?"

"I suppose so. I can't really tell one horse from another."

"He looks pretty frisky," her father said.

"Yeah, that's why we're longeing him," Marcy said. "Let him get it out of his system before I get on. I don't want to get bucked off."

"Bucked off?" her mother asked. "Surely there's no danger of that? I thought you said he was—what did you say?"

"Broke. Quiet." Marcy said in a small voice. "And he *was* out at Foggy Creek when I tried him, but . . . but . . ."

"Oh, he's just feeling good," Sasha said. "Wind always makes horses skittery, and this is a new place. He'll settle down."

Marcy looked at Sasha gratefully and hoped that she was right. She'd rather leave rodeoing to T.C. and his friend, Hoyt. Richard bucked and kicked and snorted, having a fine old time, but at last he settled back to a canter, just shaking his head or kicking up his heels now and then.

"There," Sasha said. "See?"

Marcy nodded, keeping one eye on Richard, wondering if he would explode again.

"What do you think of him?" her father asked Sasha.

"Marcy and T.C. made a real find," she said. "He's got good conformation and he's a good mover."

"What does that mean?"

"Well, the way a horse is put together will affect his ability to perform. Now, you see the angle of his croup? . . ." Sasha went on, pointing out the features in Richard's physical makeup that indicated he would be an athletic type of horse.

Marcy's father and mother were listening to Sasha and watching Richard with the slightly vague air people assume when they don't really understand something. Marcy smiled to herself; it clearly sounded esoteric to her parents, but *she* knew what Sasha was talking about. She had learned a lot.

By the time Sasha was finished explaining the rudiments of conformation, Richard had dropped back to a trot. Nat even had to cluck and shake the whip at him once or twice to keep him from slowing to a walk.

"Why don't you hop on now," Sasha said, "and we'll see what he can do over fences."

Trying to look calm, Marcy got on and started trotting. In the far end of the ring, where he hadn't been yet, she could feel him tense up, so she circled in that end until he relaxed. After she had worked him in both directions, Sasha set up a crossrail and Marcy trotted back and forth over it. As at Foggy Creek, when she started out she was nervous, but after Richard had jumped a few fences nicely she calmed down. She stopped worrying about what her parents might be thinking and began to enjoy herself.

"Okay, good," Sasha said. "How about a course?"

"But I've only done gymnastics and lines," Marcy said. "I've never jumped a whole course."

"I know," Sasha said, "but you look fine. I think you're ready and I'll bet your parents would like to see what Richard can do."

"Would you?" Marcy asked, looking over at her mother and father.

"Well, sure, Marshmallow," her father said. "That's what you got him for, isn't it?"

Marcy nodded. "Nat did a course on him when we were out at Foggy Creek on Tuesday. You should have seen him!" she exclaimed. "Snappy with his knees, and round! He really—"

"Okay, Marcy," Sasha said, "here's the course. Start over the brush, then do that line on the far side— the vertical to the stone wall . . ." After she'd finished outlining the course, she had Marcy repeat it, to get it fixed in her mind.

Then Marcy was cantering a circle, the way she'd seen people do at the show, and heading for the first fence. She was jumping a course, and on her very own horse! When she jumped the last fence, she finished off with another circle, pulled Richard up and walked over to Sasha, beaming.

"Very nice," Sasha said. "All the work you've been doing is beginning to pay off."

"Isn't he an angel?" Marcy asked. "I've never jumped a whole course before and he did it like it was old hat."

Sasha smiled. "No doubt it is, for him. That's just what you need—a horse that knows what he's doing."

"What about that schooling show at Jackson's Ranch?" Marcy asked. "Can I go?"

"Maybe," Sasha said. "Let's give it a little time. See how you two settle in with each other."

"That was great!" her father said. "You looked wonderful flying over those jumps."

"You certainly did," her mother said. "I'm proud of you."

"Thanks," Marcy said. "I just knew he was going to be my lucky horse."

"I would like him no matter how many socks he had," Sasha said.

"Well, maybe," Marcy said, "but I'm glad he only has one."

Sasha invited Marcy's parents up to the house for a glass of tea and Marcy and Nat took Richard back to the barn to untack him and get him cleaned up.

While Marcy worked on one side, Nat worked on the other. Marcy brushed with strong circular sweeps of the currycomb, and caked-on mud and dirt came off in clouds.

"Did you hear what my mother said?" Marcy asked.

"I heard," Nat said.

"I can't believe it. She said I did a good job. She said she was proud of me."

Nat banged the currycomb on the bottom of her boot and looked at Marcy thoughtfully. "Promise you won't get mad if I say something?"

"Promise."

"Sometimes I think you make your mother into a witch on purpose, just so you'll have something to complain about."

"I do not!"

"You promised."

"You don't understand."

"What don't I understand? I think your mother's nice."

"Oh, sure. She's nice to everyone else. It's just me—"

"Marce, didn't you *hear* her?"

"Yeah, but . . ."

"Why don't you believe what she said?"

"Because she keeps making cracks about playing the piano, like . . . like . . . that's the most important thing in the world, and it's not okay that I like riding better. She just doesn't understand me."

"Oh, pooh," Nat said, "that's just one of your cherished illusions. No one can understand anyone else. Not really. You're the only one who lives in your skin. You have to understand yourself and not expect other people to do it for you."

Marcy went back to brushing Richard. That was a lot simpler than carrying on this conversation. She took up the stiff brush and worked so hard on Richard's coat that he pinned his ears back and turned his head to give her a menacing look. She lightened the pressure and brushed along his neck, moving along to his sides and legs. All that brushing didn't turn her brain off, though. Maybe Nat was right. Maybe her mother really was proud of her. Could it be, then, that she herself was the one who didn't understand?

"Well, now," T.C. said, "how's it going?"

Marcy jumped. "Oh, hi, T.C. I didn't hear you."

"Just knocked off work," T.C. said, "and thought I'd come out to see what you was doin'. How are you getting along with your new baby?"

"Fine," Marcy said, "I just jumped a whole course on him and he was an absolute angel, wasn't he Nat?"

"Yeah, you should have seen him, T.C. He's a really good jumper and unflappable. These fences are all new to him, and he didn't dig in his toes to look or anything. Pretty soon Marcy's going to give me a run for the money."

Marcy was going to protest, then she remembered that Sasha had told Nat she had a natural feel, and if she kept on working, especially now that she had her own horse and could really put in the hours, well . . .

"He's pretty cute, all right," T.C. was saying, "and he's lookin' a damn sight better already. Before you know it he'll be as fat and sleek and pretty as a show horse."

"Yeah, well, he better, because that's what he's going to be, aren't you, Richard?"

"Is that what you're goin' to call him when you take him to a show?"

Marcy stopped brushing Richard for a minute and turned around to look at T.C. "Funny you should ask. I've been thinking about show names. Thinking and *thinking*, but I haven't come up with anything. I never had any trouble thinking of names for my fantasy horses, but now that I have a real one I can't think of a thing. Got any ideas?"

"Well, let see . . . How 'bout Upside Down?"

"Upside Down?" Marcy echoed vaguely.

"Sure," T.C. said. "I can hear it now: 'And now on course is number two hundred and one. This is Marcy Connolly riding Upside Down!' "

Nat giggled.

"Not funny," Marcy said. "I'd rather be right side up, thank you."

"How about In a Roast Beef Sandwich?" Nat suggested.

"Yeah," T.C. said, slapping his thigh.

"That's terrific," Marcy said, "but I think Under the Table would be better."

"Or N.P. Soup? Nat offered.

"That would be good for a gray. Why don't you change Joey's name to that, since you think it's so funny?"

"Okay, and you could name Richard 'Blind.' Then you'll be riding blind and I'll be in pea soup."

"Seriously now," T.C. said, "you might call him Mahogany. He's going to be a real pretty mahogany color when he sheds out."

"Yeah," Marcy said. "Mahogany Prince? Mahogany Serenade?"

"Sounds a little high falutin' to me," T.C. said, "but I'm just a country boy."

Nat wrinkled her nose. "A little schmaltzy."

Marcy sighed. "We don't seem to be getting very far."

"Well, I'm plumb out of ideas," T.C. said. He stepped back and gave Richard the horse-looking-at look.

"Yep, he's a real nice horse. Seems like he was worth waiting for. Well, I reckon I'll mosey along. My stomach says it's supper time."

T.C. was only a little way down the path when Marcy's brush strokes got slower and slower and then stopped all together. "That's it!" she yelled. "T.C.! That's IT!"

T.C. stopped and turned around. "Good Lord, honey, I'm only a few yards down the path, not halfway across the Golden Gate Bridge. What's it?' "

"The name! You did it! You just gave Richard his show name!"

"Aw, I was just funnin'. I don't think you should call him Upside Down or any of them others. Too silly."

"No, not those, but what you just said—that he was worth waiting for. You're right, and that's what I'm going to call him—Worth Waiting. Doesn't that sound good?"

"Not bad," T.C. said.

"Not *bad*? I think it's great, don't you Nat?"

"Yeah, it is good. I like it," Nat replied.

"Well, I'm glad I said somethin' useful," T.C. said.

"Me too. You did a lot. Finding him and all. How can I ever thank you?"

"No need," T.C. said. "It was my pleasure." He tipped his cap with a jaunty gesture and headed on down the path.

Marcy turned back to Richard. "You sure were worth waiting for," she told him.

Chapter 14

MARCY WAS GLAD the next day was Saturday. She'd have plenty of time to ride, give Richard a bath, then she and Nat could take their horses out to eat grass and laze around. When Marcy walked down the barn aisle toward Richard's stall he whickered at her.

"How's my good boy today?" she asked.

He looked at her as if to say, "Fine, what's up?"

"We're going for a ride," Marcy said. "How does that sound? I'd like to take you for a trail ride, but it would probably be better if we worked in the ring for a while. We need to get used to each other. What do you say?"

Richard's ears flicked forward at the sound of her voice and he nuzzled her hand with his muzzle.

Marcy rode him into the ring to practice some of the things she had been working on in her lessons. After she had walked around a few times to get Richard loosened up, she started trotting, doing an exercise to perfect her balance. She would get up in a half-seat, the jumping position, for three beats of the trot, then post three, trying to keep her legs still and the angle of her upper body the same. When she had first done this she had had to grab mane, her legs had wiggled all over the place, and she felt as if she were constantly out of balance. Now she felt the weight go firmly down into her heels and her upper body stayed still, poised fluidly out of the saddle. As they were turning the far corner of the ring a deer came bounding out of the woods and Richard shied. Marcy stayed right with him, didn't even think about using her hands for balance. She grinned. I'm getting it together, she thought, I really am.

She did another exercise at the trot: five steps of sitting trot, five of posting, five in a half-seat. Around and around the ring she went, counting, losing herself in the steady two-beat rhythm of the trot. Then she dropped her stirrups and did the same thing without stirrups. She looked at her watch first because riding without stirrups had a way of seeming endless. When she thought she had been working without stirrups for at least fifteen minutes, she would look at her watch and discover that it had been only five. At first she had done ten minutes without stirrups every day. For the last month she'd been doing fifteen. She decided to increase it to twenty in celebration of Richard's arrival.

She varied the routine; she didn't want Richard getting bored while she was working on her equitation. She switched to a straight sitting trot and tried to drive him up into the bit with her legs. She closed her eyes and focused on feeling his hind legs moving beneath her, trying to make them move farther forward under his body without increasing the pace. She didn't want him to go faster, all strung out, leaning on his forehand; she wanted to create more impulsion, to get him into a frame. She played with the bit, used her legs, and gradually he softened. She felt as if she had all of him under control. He was alert and ready to do whatever she asked, when she asked. She inched her leg back and squeezed. As soon as she gave the signal he struck off into a canter, balanced and smooth. Marcy smiled. Transitions were much easier when he was on the bit.

She did a half-turn and asked for a flying change of lead, but he cantered on, still on the right lead. She dropped back to a trot and asked for the left lead. He took it perfectly, but when she reversed and asked for a flying change again, he still didn't do it. Marcy sighed. She would have to be able to do flying changes if she expected to get anywhere at a show. And she was hoping to go to that schooling show at Jackson's Ranch, only three weeks away. Well, she must be doing something wrong. She'd ask Sasha to help her in her next lesson.

She looked at her watch and nearly fell off in surprise. She'd been riding for thirty-five minutes without stirrups! She'd even forgotten that she didn't have her stirrups, she'd been thinking so much about keeping him on the bit and getting him to bend correctly. Well, that was enough for one day. She let him walk on a loose rein while she turned her feet in circles and shook her legs to relax the muscles.

He was pretty hot, and she walked until he wasn't blowing any more. When she rode to the barn, Nat had a bucket of hot water ready. They washed him all over with shampoo, then they took the hose and rinsed him off. After his bath, they scraped off the excess water with the metal scraper and put a net cooler on him and, over that, a wool cooler. He looked like a great big baby wrapped up in a bunting.

Marcy walked him until he was dry, then she put him in the crossties to give him a thorough grooming. When she brushed out his mane and tail, they shone almost blue black in the lowering sun. Marcy brushed his tail until none of the strands stuck together, and when she held it out it cascaded down like a fan of fine silk threads. She let the hairs swish back and forth in her fingers, thinking that she had never felt anything so fine.

"Where's Sasha?" she asked. "I wish she could see how much better he looks."

Nat shrugged. "She's out in her studio, I guess, or somewhere with Jim."

"How come he wasn't here yesterday? He said he wanted to see Richard."

"How should I know? Nobody ever tells me what's going on."

Nat took the sponge and dipped it in the bucket of water, rubbed it on the bar of saddle soap and started cleaning her saddle. "He won't come to see Richard anyway. He doesn't care about us."

Marcy took the soft brush and started on Richard's neck. "He does too! He'll come. You'll see."

Nat didn't answer, but scrubbed at her saddle as if it hadn't been cleaned in a year. When she was finished she took it into the tack room. Soon Marcy heard bangs and scrapes coming from inside.

"What are you doing in there?" she called.

"Cleaning up. This place is a mess."

"Wait a minute and I'll help you."

"No. You go ahead and finish with Richard. This tack room looks like a junkyard. Look at that!" A wadded up blanket came sailing through the door.

"Quit it!" Marcy yelled. "You're scaring Richard."

"Oh, so what?" Nat said as she threw another blanket. "Just look at those. Filthy and covered with mouse turds."

"What you need is a cat."

"We need more than that!"

Clouds of dust came out of the tack room door as Nat swept the floor. Even the broom sounded angry. Marcy kept grooming Richard, trying to ignore the sounds in the tack room. When she was finished, she put Richard's blanket on and took him to his stall. When she came back to the tack room Nat was bent over the big show trunk, pulling things out of it.

"Look at that," Nat said, pointing to a pile of bits

on the floor. "For someone who believes in the snaffle bit you wonder why she's got all those. Twisted wires, Pelhams. And look at that," she said, holding up a strange-looking bit. "A gag bit! Ugh. I don't think she's cleaned this out for a hundred years." She kicked the pile of bits over into the corner.

"It's not that bad," Marcy said.

"It's a mess! I'll hang up every one of those bits and see what she says then," Nat said. She picked up a can of nails and the hammer and started pounding nails into the wall. "I'll put some to hang the girths on, too. And the longe line," Nat mumbled, pounding furiously.

"Nat!"

"And my chaps. And these extra halters," Nat said, ignoring Marcy. "Take that," she muttered, swinging at a nail. "And that!" She pulled the hammer way past her shoulder and swung it at the nail as if she were wielding an axe. Whap!

"Owww!" she yelled, hopping up and down with her thumb in her mouth.

"Let's see," Marcy said.

Nat held out her thumb.

"It looks okay to me," Marcy said.

"It doesn't *feel* okay," Nat said, bursting into tears. She buried her head in her hands and cried.

Marcy couldn't think of anything to say, so she put her arm around her and patted her shoulder the way her mother did when she was upset.

When her sobs subsided Marcy took Nat's hand

and inspected her thumb. "How does it feel now?" she asked.

Nat shrugged. "It's all right."

"What were you crying for, then?"

"You know," Nat said, looking at her darkly.

"No, I don't."

Nat sat down on the tack trunk and stared at Marcy. "You really don't, do you?"

Marcy shook her head.

"Well, I guess you wouldn't. You have a mother *and* a father. A family. You don't know what it's like to have your life be in flux all the time. Changing, changing. To have a crazy artist for a mother who doesn't give a damn about you. Always taking up with some man or another."

"Nat!"

"Well, it's true. Go ahead. Tell me it's not."

Marcy bit her lip.

"Yeah, see? She never even talks to me anymore. She just talks to Jim. Even when he's not there, it's Jim this, Jim that, as if he were the only person in the whole world."

"Well, he is pretty neat," Marcy said.

"Aaaargh. Not you too!"

"Well, he is."

"Oh, sure. Great."

"Couldn't you at least try to like him?"

"Why should I? It will just be like Daniel. At first I didn't like him either, but after a while I did. We used to have so much fun together . . ."

"So what's wrong with that?"

"Because he left, mushbrain, he left! So why should I try to like Jim? He'll just leave too."

"But you don't know that."

"Oh yes I do. All the others have, so why won't he? I don't care anyway. I hate him *and* her!"

Much as Marcy sometimes didn't like her mother, she would never say that she hated her. She glanced sideways at Nat, hoping that the outburst was over. Then she went over to the pile of bits on the floor and started picking them up. Nat came over, and they worked in silence hanging the bits on the nails Nat had hammered into the wall.

"It doesn't matter, anyway," Nat said after a while, "because . . ."

Marcy had never seen Nat in such a volatile mood. She held tightly onto the bit she had in her hands, as if she had been shipwrecked and it was a life preserver. She had an intuition that she didn't want to hear the rest of the "because," and when Nat said it, Marcy knew that her intuition was right.

"Because I'm leaving," Nat concluded.

"Leaving?" Marcy echoed weakly.

"Yes! I can't stand living here any longer. I'm going to live with my father." Nat said triumphantly.

"But . . . but . . ." Now Marcy felt like crying. What if Nat really did leave? Then what would Marcy do? And Joey. What about Joey? So many horrible possibilities were roiling around in her head that she couldn't say anything except, "But . . . but . . ."

"But, nothing!" Nat yelled. "I'm leaving. Then she'll be sorry."

"But I thought you said he was a . . . a no-good bum. And you don't even know where he lives."

"That's what *she* said, but why should I believe her? She's a hypocrite. And I'll find him, you'll see."

"She is not! She's nice."

"Nice," Nat hissed. "A lot you know about it. *You* have a normal family."

"Well," Marcy said finally, "I guess I don't know what it's like."

"You sure as hell don't," Nat said. She picked up the can of nails and started pounding them in again.

Marcy stood in the doorway, unsure about what to do next. Nat had her back turned, and Marcy could feel the waves of anger emitting from Nat's vicinity. "I guess I'll go home now," she said, at last.

Nat didn't answer. *Whap, whap*, went the hammer.

"Nat?"

"*What!*"

"I said I thought I'd go along home now."

Nat turned and gave her a black look. "So what? You want my permission or something?"

"No. I just . . . I just wanted to say goodbye."

"Well, fine. Goodbye." She turned and started hammering again.

Whap! Whap!

Chapter 15

FOR THE NEXT few days Nat hardly spoke to Marcy.
In the mornings, if Marcy stopped by to walk to school
with her, Nat would already be gone, and at lunchtime
she sat down at a table with only one empty place, so
Marcy had to sit with someone else. In the afternoons
at the barn, Nat went around with her head down, not
looking at Marcy, hardly speaking to her. A typical conversation went like this:

Marcy: Do you know where the hoofpick is?

Nat: On the nail, where it always is.

Marcy: No, it isn't. I looked.

Nat: Silence.

One day Marcy couldn't find the hoofpick anywhere, and she had to put Richard away without picking out his feet. If he got thrush or something, it would be Nat's fault.

More often than not, however, Marcy didn't see Nat at all in the afternoons. When she arrived at the barn Nat and Joey would be gone on a trail ride, and Marcy would ride and do all her barn work before Nat returned. Marcy had thought everything was going to be great once she had her own horse, but now she realized it wasn't just riding she liked, it was being with Nat too. It wasn't working out the way she'd planned at all. She did what she had to at the barn as fast as she could, then went home to do her homework and practice the piano.

Going home felt like a relief, and Marcy drifted up to her room, singing under her breath. If Nat were there, they could sing together—or she could sing to Nat, which Nat liked better. When Marcy had tried to get Nat to join the choir, Nat said she was allergic to church. Also, Marcy had to admit, she wasn't much of a singer. She had a pleasant voice and she could sing the melody, but when they tried to do two-part harmonies, Nat would get off and end up singing the part that Marcy was singing. Marcy couldn't understand it—harmonies were so easy, so much fun. They worked on it, but Nat really couldn't do it. She said she wished she could sing, and maybe in some other life she'd be a singer, but in this one she'd just be a "harp listener." On the way into her room Marcy paused and looked at the harp Nat had given her still hanging on the wall beside the story of

"True Friends." Who ever heard of a true friend who would hardly even speak to you? Or listen to you? And what had she done to deserve it?

After another week, Marcy couldn't stand it any more. One afternoon, while Nat was out on a trail ride, Marcy went out to Sasha's studio. Marcy hadn't seen much of her either. She'd come out to give Marcy a lesson, then she'd go back to the house or out to her studio or somewhere with Jim instead of staying around to talk the way she usually did. Sasha was bending over the lathe, wearing the old striped overalls she always wore when she was working. Marcy stood in the doorway watching for a long time: The whine of the lathe drowned out any other sounds, and Sasha's whole body was tense with concentration. Finally she straightened up, took the piece of wood she was working on and held it up, turning it this way and that.

"Oh, hi, Marcy. I didn't see you come in."

"You were working. I didn't want to startle you," Marcy yelled over the noise of the machine.

Sasha switched it off. "There. Now we can hear ourselves think. What's up?"

Marcy swallowed. She'd hardly ever talked to Sasha when Nat was not there too, and suddenly she felt bashful. "Well, I guess I'm not going to be keeping Richard here any more and and I thought I ought to tell you."

"Not keep Richard here? Where will you take him?"

"Over to McArthur's."

"But that's just a pasture! You don't want Richard to get kicked or have to fight for his food with the other horses, do you? And there's no ring there, no shelter." She stopped abruptly and peered at Marcy. "Now what would you want to move him over there for?"

"I was talking to Annie Barker at school today. She keeps her horse there. She said they have gymkhanas and cookouts and stuff. It sounds like fun."

"You really think so?"

"More fun than here!" Marcy burst out.

Sasha sighed. "That's what I thought," she said. "It hasn't been much fun around here lately, has it?"

Marcy shook her head. "I hardly ever see Nat and when I do she won't talk to me."

"She hasn't been talking to me much either, but I didn't realize that it was affecting you as well."

"Well, it is!"

Sasha picked up the piece she'd been working on and slid her fingers absently up and down the grain of wood. "Do you have any idea what's going on?" she asked.

Marcy shook her head. Even if Nat wasn't speaking to her, she still wasn't going to rat on her.

"You two have a fight or something?"

Marcy shook her head again. This time it was because she didn't trust herself to speak. All of a sudden she realized that she missed Nat, she *really* missed her, and Sasha was looking at her so sympathetically it made her want to cry.

"I think it's time I talked to her," Sasha said.

"Maybe I can get to the bottom of this." Then, after a pause, she continued quietly, almost as if she were talking to herself. "I, uh. I've been kind of preoccupied. Forgive me."

"Sure," Marcy said.

"Good," Sasha said with a smile, "and what do you say I give you a lesson tomorrow. I think we should go to that schooling show at Jackson's Ranch. Time to see what you can do under pressure."

"You really think I'm ready?" Marcy asked, feeling a glimmer of excitement. She guessed it was time for her and Richard to try their wings, and two weeks ago she would have been *really* excited, but now . . .

"You're ready," Sasha said, "I'll see you tomorrow."

As Marcy was heading down the drive, Jim's car turned in. He rolled down the window and said, "Hi, Marcy, how are you?"

"Okay, I guess."

"You guess? You mean you don't know?"

"Nope."

"Doesn't sound too positive."

"I guess not. Well, I have to go ride Richard now."

"Okay," Jim said, "see you later."

Marcy watched him drive up to the house and go inside, as if he lived there. She tried to imagine what it would be like if her mother met "some man" and he started taking her out and coming over and . . . and . . . sleeping with her. But she couldn't do it, because if her mother was doing that, where would her father be? They went together, mother-and-father, parents. She sighed. Nat was right. She didn't have the foggiest idea what it would be like.

THE NEXT MORNING Marcy set off for school going the "old" route, the street way that she'd had to take when the Donaldsons wouldn't let her cut through their yard. She'd been going that way all week, giving Nat the space she seemed to want. If Nat didn't want to talk to her, or walk to school with her, then she'd just walk by herself.

As she was turning the corner someone jumped out behind her and said, "Boo!"

Marcy jumped and screamed, "Oh!"

"Scared you, didn't I?" Nat asked.

"Yep," Marcy answered cautiously.

"Boy, did I have to get up early. I've been sitting here for hours waiting for you."

Marcy gave her a sidelong glance and waited.

"I talked to Sasha last night."

"So?"

"Oh, she said a bunch of stuff. You know, she reminded me of your mother—she sounded so . . . so much like a mother. And then she said that you were going to move Richard to McArthur's," Nat said. "It's not true is it? Marcy, you *can't* leave! That place is a real dump."

"Well, you said you were going to leave, so I thought: I can leave too. Annie Barker said they go on group trail rides there, and on the last Saturday of every month they have a gymkhana and a barbeque. Doesn't that sound like fun?"

"Annie Barker, blek. Since when were you so cozy with her?"

"I have to eat lunch with someone. Anyway, what do you care? I thought *you* were leaving."

"I am, but not until summer. And this is only February. It's a long time until June."

Marcy gulped. She hadn't really believed that Nat would leave. Finding her father and going to live with him had sounded like a crazy dream. "But what about Joey? We were going to go to lots of shows this summer and take the horses out to Point Reyes to ride on the beach, and, and . . . what about your medals? You were going to try to qualify for the Medal and the Maclay, remember? Ride in the finals."

Nat shrugged. "There are more important things than medals, and I've been going to horse shows practically all my life. This summer I'm going to do something different. I'm going to live with my father on his boat!"

Marcy was stunned. Ever since she bought Richard, she'd been thinking about the summertime when she could ride all day long if she wanted to. Sasha had a calendar from the Pacific Coast Hunter and Jumper Association with all the shows listed in it. Marcy and Nat had looked at it and talked about which shows they might go to. And she'd missed Nat so much these past two weeks, the thought of her going away for a whole summer was almost more than she could bear. She walked along with her shoulders sagging while her mind veered away from what Nat was saying. All her plans for the summer included Nat—and Joey. Nat and Joey, Marcy and Richard.

Nat didn't even notice that Marcy wasn't responding. She was rattling on about her father. He lived on a big sailboat in Hawaii and chartered the boat out to people who wanted to cruise the islands. He was going to make Nat his first mate and teach her all about the winds and the tides, how to use a sextant and navigate by the stars. "And when there aren't any charters, he said we would go island-hopping by ourselves, just the two of us. We'll take off," Nat said, excitement edging into her voice, "with the whole ocean before us and a fair wind in the sails. Oh, it's going to be glorious!"

"That sounds great," Marcy said sourly, "and you found him just like that? After all these years?"

"Oh sure," Nat said, with a wave of her hand. "Piece of cake."

"But what about Joey? You can't just abandon him."

"You'll take care of him while I'm gone, won't you? Just think, you can have two horses to show instead of just one."

"If you want," Marcy said dully. "But it won't be much fun without you. And what about our harps? I thought we were true friends."

"Who said that we weren't?"

Marcy sighed. Life with Nat was hardly ever dull,

the way it sometimes had been with Susan, but sometimes she wished that Nat's family was just a teeny bit like the Appelbaum's—or Marcy's own. Nothing exotic ever happened at their house, but at least you could *count* on them. And Marcy thought that being true friends meant, also, being everyday friends, and that wasn't possible if one of you went batting off to Hawaii.

"Anyway," Nat said, "it's going to be *exciting*. It's a bore staying in the same place all the time."

"Six months sure doesn't seem like 'all the time.' "

Nat threw her arm around Marcy's shoulders. "Don't be such an old sourpuss, and just wait 'til I tell you what Sasha said last night."

Marcy thought she recognized the tone. It was going to be something wild, something she probably didn't want to hear.

"There's no point in holding grudges, you know," Nat said. "You've got to be open and honest with your feelings. Otherwise, you just turn them in on yourself and get angry or depressed."

Marcy giggled and sighed with relief at the same time. So far it wasn't too bad.

"What's so funny?"

"You sound like Old Ronzo Garbanzo."

"Yeah, you should have seen us. Last night Sasha and Jim and I sat down and had a rap session that even she would approve of. You know, I was wrong about Jim. He's really pretty nice."

"See? Didn't I tell you?"

"Yeah. Sasha said stuff like I figured she would.

That she has her own life to lead, and that she . . . she loves Jim, but she didn't want to hurt me, and she really loves me too. It would be much better for all of us if we could be open about our feelings, work out any problems and not let things just fester inside. It got sort of mushy, but, anyway, I do feel better. And Jim said that he wasn't planning to leave, but he couldn't be sure what the future would bring, so he couldn't *promise* anything. Meanwhile, he thought it would be a lot better if I didn't judge him on the basis of what someone else did in the past."

"So if everything's so great at your house, how come you're going to leave? And how come Sasha's going to let you go and stay with your father? I thought she didn't think much of him."

Nat suddenly looked evasive. "Oh well—she said, uh, that maybe it was time in my development to confront the father. Anyway, that's in the future. You know the song, 'One Day at a Time?' "

Marcy nodded.

"Jim said he tried to live like that and maybe it would help if I did too."

"Yeah," Marcy said, starting to sing: " 'One day at a time, just live one day at a time. Yesterday is gone and tomorrow is blind.' "

Nat joined in and they sang the rest of the way to school.

Chapter 16

FOR THE REST of the week all Marcy could think about was the schooling show they were planning to attend on Sunday. Once in a while she would see an image of Nat at the wheel of a sailboat, her hair like skeins of saffron, caught by the sun, wisping in the wind. In front of her, white sails bloomed with a fair wind, and beside her stood a tall, attractive man with blond hair who handed her a coconut. Nat took a sip of coconut milk, then handed it back to him. They laughed together, their teeth very white in their tanned faces, Nat's clear soprano blending with the deeper tones of the man. And the boat skimmed across the blue water, cavorting like a dolphin through the waves . . . Marcy didn't like this image at all. She hoped that his boat would sink with him in it. Then she and Nat could ride together all summer long, and she wouldn't have to take care of Joey as well as Richard. She'd just learned how to cope with one horse; she wasn't at all sure that she could manage two.

But, "living one day at a time" meant not thinking too far into the future. It meant riding after school, which Marcy enjoyed again, now that Nat was not sulking any more. They giggled over funny things that Joey and Richard did and spent time, the way they used to, gossiping about what happened at school and planning for the show. When she was riding, Marcy worked harder than usual, thinking about the show, trying to improve her performance and Richard's.

Earlier in the week she'd sat down with Sasha to go over the prize list. Sasha marked the classes she thought Marcy should enter: Warm-up Hunters, with fences two feet six inches to two feet nine inches, Green Working Hunters with fences two feet nine inches to three feet, Maiden Equitation Over Fences for riders seventeen and under, and Novice Hunters. Those were jumping classes. On the flat she had Hunters Under Saddle and Maiden Equitation.

"What does 'Maiden' mean?" Marcy asked.

"It means that the people in that class have never won a blue ribbon in that division."

"And Novice?"

"It means they haven't won three. Or the horse hasn't, if it's a class where the horse is being judged."

"Do you really think I can do it?" Marcy asked. "Ride in a show? With people watching and a judge looking, writing down everything I do wrong?"

"Or right," Sasha said. "Think positively. And, sure, I think you can do it. You're ready."

As Sunday approached, Marcy found herself getting more and more excited. She was going to a show! Wouldn't it be wonderful if she won a class? Then she could put the trophy on her bookshelf, like Nat did, and hang the ribbon on the wall over her bed. A blue ribbon would look lovely on her wall.

The night before the show Marcy was so excited she couldn't eat dinner. And after dinner she couldn't sit still. She took out the prize list again. She'd marked the classes she had entered with an M and the ones Nat was going in with an N. During the week she'd looked at it so often it was creased and tattered. She folded up the prize list and put it back in her pocket. She paced around the house, stopped in front of the TV and turned it on. She looked at the people on the screen gesticulating, talking. They looked absurd, sounded absurd. Marcy changed the channel. Same thing. She turned the TV off. She opened a book, shut it. Then she went up to her room to look at the icon of St. Demetrius, which Nat had lent her for luck. She stood in front of it for a long time looking into his dreamy eyes, but he didn't give her the peaceful feeling he usually did. She started pacing again. Finally, she went to the telephone and called Sasha and told her that she was sick and she wouldn't be able to go to the show.

"Nonsense," Sasha said. "You've got the jitters. I'll see you in the morning at six o'clock sharp."

When her alarm clock went off at five-thirty the next morning, the first thing Marcy did was go to the window to see what the weather was like. It was still dark, but she could tell that it wasn't raining. A few stars glowed dimly in the sky and the air felt fresh and cool, as if it would be a clear and pleasant day.

By the time they pulled into the showgrounds it was light, and there were already several other trailers parked on a grassy field across the road from the big ring where the show was to be held. People were bustling around unloading their horses and getting them ready for the first class. Things got so busy Marcy didn't have time to be nervous. She had to get Richard out of the trailer, clean him up, put his tack on and warm up.

After she'd warmed up in the schooling ring and was standing outside the big ring waiting for her turn, it hit her with a jolt. Her stomach was jumping up and down so much that, if there'd been anything in it she would have thrown up. She stood near the in-gate looking at the jumps in the ring. There were post-and-rail oxers and verticals and a coop and a brush like they had at home. There was also a solid wooden jump painted to look like a brick wall. When Marcy saw that her heart went flipflop. She'd never jumped such a thing before.

"Oh, look at that cute little wall," someone behind her said.

Cute *little* wall! It looked huge to Marcy. She was sure she would never get over it.

"Yeah, and isn't that coop darling?" the girl's friend. "Oooh, this is going to be so much fun."

Marcy's mind went blank. Inside her gloves her hands were sweating.

"Marce, do you know the course?" Sasha asked.

"No." Marcy choked. "But I won't have to jump that wall, will I?"

"Sure. It's part of the course."

"But it's so huge! And I've never jumped anything like that before. Can't I just leave it out?"

Sasha laughed. "Certainly not. The first thing you've got to do is jump all the fences in the right order. Now, let me tell you the course." When she was finished she said, "Okay, got it?"

Marcy nodded.

"All right, tell it back to me."

"The brush. Then that vertical and . . . and . . ."

"Marcy, pay attention. Concentrate. You've done courses like this at home. It's no different."

"Yes, it is," Marcy wailed. "At home no one was watching me."

"*I* was watching you."

"That's different."

"No, it's not. Just pretend that you're at home. Now I want you to watch a few people go. That will help you to remember the course."

Marcy nodded and looked at the horse in the ring. She sat there for twenty minutes watching horses go round the course. Finally the gateman said, "Okay, I need some more people up here. If I don't have a horse in one minute, the class will be closed."

"Okay, Marce," Sasha said. "You can't put it off any longer. Time to go."

Marcy picked up her reins and headed into the ring. She cantered a circle, gritting her teeth, pointed Richard at the brush. Come on, Richard, she thought, come on!

The next thing she knew she was flat on her back looking at the sky and gasping for air. When she raised her head she saw Richard tearing around the ring bucking and squealing. She got up slowly, brushed the dirt off her pants, and stood there watching helplessly as Richard ran around and around the ring.

Several other people appeared in the ring, then, saying, "Whoa! Whoa!" and reaching for the reins as Richard galloped by. Finally, with stiff-legged, propping motions he came to a halt by the gate. The gateman grabbed the reins while Richard snorted and rolled his eyes. Marcy took the reins from him and headed out the gate. Once outside she began to shake.

"Are you all right?" Sasha asked.

"Yes. At least my body is. What happened? He's never stopped before. Why did he stop?"

"You had such a death grip on the reins he couldn't have jumped that fence no matter how much he wanted to."

"Really?"

Sasha nodded. "I could see it coming six, eight

strides away. You were so tense your face was white and you were yanking on his mouth every step of the way. His stride got shorter and shorter and you got farther and farther ahead of him. Of course he stopped. And of course you fell off."

"I feel like such a fool."

"Don't worry about it. Everyone falls off. Now get back on, and we'll go jump a few fences in the schooling ring. You've got the next class, you know."

Sasha gave her a leg up and Marcy walked over to the schooling ring. She trotted around for a minute or two and began to feel a little better. At least she remembered how to post.

"Okay," Sasha said. "Trot the X."

Marcy did it, but Richard felt tense and the jump was jerky.

"Loosen up. You've got to give him some rein."

Marcy gave him more rein and she could feel Richard relaxing. The jumps over the X began to feel better, almost like they did at home.

"Okay," Sasha said, "canter the vertical."

Marcy cantered up to the vertical, but Richard slammed on the brakes and she was teetering precariously in front of the saddle, clutching at his neck to keep from falling off again.

"What's wrong?" she wailed.

"You're too tense," Sasha said, "and you're getting ahead of him. You're not giving him a chance."

"I can't do it," Marcy said. "Let Nat do it."

"No," Sasha said. "That won't do you any good.

Now listen to me. This is no different from a lesson at home. Just canter down to that fence and stay off his mouth. Grab mane if you have to. He'll jump it if you give him half a chance."

After a few minutes of cantering back and forth Marcy began to feel a bit more confident. At least he didn't stop any more.

"All right," Sasha said, "let's go on that."

Marcy walked back over to the ring, but when she got there she didn't feel too good. What if Richard stopped again? What if she fell off?

Then the gateman called her number and she was in the ring again. This time she managed to jump the brush and the first line, which was two post-and-rail verticals, and then she turned down the middle of the ring heading for the red wall. The closer she got the bigger it looked. Ooh, ooh, ooh. Splat!

She was on the ground again. This time Richard stood close behind her with his head down, looking at her reproachfully.

Marcy took the reins in her hand and led Richard toward the gate.

"Get back on!" Sasha yelled. "Jump the brush!"

Marcy just kept walking, with her head down, watching the toes of her boots sinking into the dirt.

"Marcy, Marcy, Marcy," Sasha said, when she came out the gate.

"What?

"Don't walk out of the ring like that again. Richard will begin to realize he can get away with it."

"Well, he can."

"Only if you let him."

Marcy didn't trust herself to speak. She took Richard back to the trailer and tied him up. Then she went over to a grove of trees by the side of the ring and walked into the trees until, when she looked back, she could no longer see the ring, and she was certain that no one could see her.

She lay in the leaves staring up at the sky. Why was Sasha being so mean? Didn't she know that she was trying? She'd never been so humiliated in her life. She was the laughingstock of the whole show. The worst rider there. The worst rider anywhere.

Through the trees she heard the announcer: "Announcing the awards in this class, Green Working Hunters with fences two feet nine inches to three feet in height . . ." And last night she'd been dumb enough to imagine that this show would be fun, that she might win a ribbon or two. A *blue* ribbon. Ha! She couldn't even get around the course without falling off. She turned over on her side wondering how she could have been so stupid. She just wanted to go home and forget the whole thing.

". . . First place goes to number thirty-two, Natasha Jones riding Seaspray. Congratulations, Natasha. And in second place is . . ." So Nat won it. That figured. Another blue ribbon to put on her wall with all the others. Another trophy for her bookshelf. The announcer was calling for horses for the next class—Novice Hunters. Marcy was entered in that class, but it didn't matter. She wasn't going in the ring to make a fool out of herself again. She'd just stay where she was, watching the leaves moving overhead.

In the distance she heard the announcer calling numbers and names as horses entered the ring in the next class. Marcy wished she could transfer herself home by some magic process that would eliminate the necessity of talking to Sasha or Nat, or seeing them, or anyone else. She waited for what seemed like a long time, but nothing miraculous happened—or magical either. A cloud passed over the sun and she felt the dampness from the ground creeping into her skin. She sighed and got up. She brushed herself off and walked back to the trailer, dragging her feet.

Richard was tied where she had left him, but someone had untacked him and given him a bucket of water and a hay net.

Sasha came around from the other side of the tailer. "Where have you been?" she asked.

"For a walk."

"Well, let me tell you something: No matter what, your horse comes first. It is *not okay* to leave him like that, with no water, no food, without even loosening the girth or taking off his bridle."

"But I was upset!"

"I don't care how upset you were. Don't you ever do that again. It wasn't his fault."

"I know. It's me. I'm a failure.

"Oh, pooh. So you had a little trouble in the first two classes, so what? It's not the end of the world."

"Maybe. But I don't want to do this anymore. I want to go home."

"And do what?"

Marcy bit her lip.

"Lie on your bed and feel sorry for yourself?"

"No," she lied, "I'm just not ready for this. I can't do it. Besides, I feel really sick," she concluded, clutching her stomach.

"Everyone has nerves and the way to conquer them is to get in there and do it. That's the only way you'll ever get any confidence."

"It doesn't make me feel confident when all I ever do is fall off."

"You only fell off twice. That's nothing. I couldn't even count the number of times I've fallen off. It's all part of the game. And you're still in one piece. No harm done. The first three fences you did in that second class were not bad. Now all you have to do is go in there and do five more, just like those."

"Fat chance," Marcy snorted.

"Okay, fine," Sasha said, looking disgusted. "Go ahead. Throw in the towel. Quit. Take Richard back to Foggy Creek, or over to McArthur's. It's no skin off my back."

Marcy didn't answer and Sasha turned and walked off toward the ring.

Marcy sat down beside the truck, scraping her boot back and forth in the grass. Other horses and riders left their trailers and went up to the ring, looking shiny and neat, all dressed up, ready for a performance. Marcy sat absently hitting the side of her boot with her crop. *Throw in the towel. Quit.* Sasha's words echoed in her mind. Marcy groaned and wished she could do something to make it go away. *Quit. Quit.*

"No, I won't," she said at last. "Maybe I quit dancing, but I'm not going to quit this. Dana wouldn't quit and dancing is a lot easier. She only has herself to contend with. I have myself and my horse." She looked at Richard speculatively. "What do you say, Richard? You want to go belly up? Throw in the towel? Go home?" She waited, hoping for a sign from him, but he simply looked at her and told her nothing. "All right," she muttered, "I guess I have to decide this one for myself —and I've decide that we're going to do it. Hear that? We're going to do it!" She jumped up and gave Richard a slap on the rump. Then she fixed her hair, put Richard's saddle and bridle on, and rode up to the ring. I may not get any curtain calls, she thought, but this is it. The performance I've been wanting and waiting for, and I'm going to do it. I'm *not* going to quit. Not this time.

Sasha and Nat were leaning on the rail talking to a woman with dark hair whom Marcy didn't know.

"Decided to join the party?" Sasha asked.

Marcy nodded.

"All right. Go trot around in the schooling ring and I'll be there in a minute."

Was Sasha pleased? Marcy couldn't be sure, but she thought she detected a hint of a smile, something in her expression that made Marcy believe she'd made the right decision. Sasha wasn't angry. She just wanted her to do well. Didn't she? Probably, Marcy thought. Then she patted Richard. Anyway, it's what *I* want. It's what you want too, isn't it, Richard? He turned his head and nuzzled her boot, went, "Snuff, snuff," with a soft whuffling noise, the way he did when Marcy came to get him in the afternoon. At last! A sign from him too.

When Sasha arrived she said, "Okay, trot the X. We don't have much time. The class is nearly over."

Marcy trotted the X a few times and all was well, but when she cantered up to the vertical Richard stopped.

"Hit him!" Sasha said. "Get after him!"

"But it's my fault!" Marcy wailed. "He never stopped before."

"He's just figured out that he can. Now get after him!"

Marcy hit him with her crop.

"Harder! Make him feel it. Okay, there! Now he'll go. He's got to know that jumping the fence is going to be a lot less painful than not jumping it. Now canter down here again. Keep your weight in your heels, and don't get ahead of him."

Marcy took a deep breath and cantered toward the fence, trying to do what Sasha told her to.

"All right, good! See?"

Marcy nodded.

"Do it again."

She jumped the vertical several more times and then Sasha said, "Okay, you're ready."

Up at the ring Marcy watched some of the other riders jumping the course. The course had been changed, but she still had to jump the red wall. This time it was the last fence in the course, on a line four strides after a white gate.

Then it was her turn. I'm not a quitter, she told herself. I'm not. I can do it. Come on, Richard. Let's go!

Then she was in the ring again, cantering a circle. She jumped the first fence and the next and the next. Six fences and everything was fine. Now she was turning left at the far turn, heading for the white gate. They jumped that, now four strides to the red wall. One, two, three, four. Oh, no! Richard came to a screeching halt in front of the wall. Marcy sat on him looking down at the wall. She was looking *down* at it. It wasn't so big, after all.

"Hit him!" Sasha yelled. "Gallop around and jump it again!"

Marcy hit him and cantered off in a circle. Then she was heading for the wall again.

"Leg!" Sasha yelled. Marcy pressed her legs into Richard's sides and she was over it. She actually jumped the wall!

She left the ring smiling.

"See," Sasha said, "I told you you could do it." She was smiling too.

"Yeah, I did it, didn't I?"

"Umhm. I'm proud of you. That was good, determined riding."

"Do you think I'll get a ribbon?"

"Not with that refusal. That's a major fault."

Marcy sighed.

"Don't be discouraged. That was a big improvement, and you're getting experience. Mileage. That's what it takes."

"It sure is a lot harder than it looks."

"Yes, but you're getting there. Now, you've got one more class. It's your chance to put in a good round, show me what you've learned today."

"Will I have to jump that wall again?"

"No doubt. It seems to be here for the duration of the show."

Marcy wrinkled up her nose.

"You jumped it once. No reason why you can't do it again."

Chapter 17

MARCY AND NAT had a break while they ran classes for amateurs. They made sure that their horses were comfortable, then walked up to the ring to watch. Nat bought some juice and a sandwich, but Marcy didn't feel like eating anything.

"You've got to eat, Marce, you need some energy."

"I've got plenty of energy, which I wouldn't have if I threw up. I'll just get something to drink."

They sat on a grassy hill above the ring sipping their drinks and talking, with one eye on what was going on in the ring. After a while, when she saw other horses refuse or run out, it began to dawn on Marcy that maybe she wasn't the worst rider at the show, after all. Other people made mistakes too.

Then it was time to swing into action again. Marcy had Maiden Equitation Over Fences and Nat had Open Working Hunters and Practice Medal Class.

"What's a practice medal class?" Marcy asked.

"They judge it like a medal class," Nat said, "with a work-off among the top four contestants, but it's a practice medal class because it's not a real medal class. You can only have those at a recognized show."

Marcy already knew that a recognized show was one that was sanctioned by the American Horse Shows Association. It had to meet certain requirements as to fence height, course design, judging, and so on, which were prescribed by the AHSA. Someday Marcy wanted to go to a show like that, but it looked like she needed more experience first. She had to laugh at herself when she remembered that she'd been hoping to go to one in January. Thinking that she was capable of it. Well, she hadn't been ready in January, and she still wasn't, but she was getting there.

When she got on and took Richard over to the warm-up ring, he felt like his old self.

"That's an improvement," Sasha said, when she'd finished warming up. "Now I want you to concentrate on the course. Don't panic. Think. Take it one part at a time, as if it were an exercise we were working on at home."

Marcy nodded and watched the course, trying to be cool and analytical instead of going off into a panic flight of nervousness. The course was almost the same as the second one she'd done in the morning. The last line was the same white gate to the red wall. Marcy sighed and wished they would leave the wall out, just once.

Then she was in the ring again. She made it over the first six fences, then she was rounding the corner, heading for the white gate. They jumped the gate, then one, two, three, four, leg, leg, leg, and they were over the wall! She'd done it! She jumped the whole course just like she was supposed to!

"Pretty good," Sasha said.

"At least he didn't stop," Marcy said. "Do you think I'll get a ribbon?"

"Well, I don't know. You got jumped a little loose over that vertical and you were pretty deep to the coop. And he was cross-cantering on the last turn."

"He was? I didn't notice."

"You were probably thinking about the dread red wall."

Marcy smiled. "I was. But you know what? When I jumped it, it didn't feel different from any of the other jumps."

"And it wasn't," Sasha said. "Ninety percent of this ballgame is mental."

When the announcer announced the awards Marcy listened with her fingers crossed, hoping that her number would be called. He called out first, second, all the way down to sixth place without calling her number. Then he said, "And reserve in this class goes to number thirty-one, Marcy Connolly, riding Worth Waiting."

"What does that mean?" she asked. "Do I get to go back in the ring? Do I get a ribbon?"

"No. It means that if there had been one more ribbon, it would have been yours."

"Phooey."

"Phooey, nothing. That means you were seventh. There were more than twenty horses in the class, so that's not bad at all. And you have two more classes. The show isn't over yet."

"Those are flat classes. I was hoping to get something over fences."

"There will be other shows. The important thing is that you learned something."

BY THE TIME the jumping classes were over it was almost four o'clock and deep shadows were creeping across the ring. Marcy walked up to the ring for her flat classes feeling remarkably calm. Working on the flat was a lot easier than jumping. The first class was Hunters Under Saddle, which meant that the horse was being judged.

"Get him on the bit," Sasha said, "get him in a nice frame and let him trot out a little. Show him off. He's a nice mover."

Marcy had never been in a ring with so many other horses. It was distracting, but she worked at keeping Richard on the bit and tried to find a place on the rail by herself, where the judge would be able to get a good look at Richard. They walked, trotted, and cantered going to the left. Then they reversed and did the same thing going to the right.

"All right," the announcer said, "come in and line up, please."

In the line-up Marcy sat up straight, jiggling the bit to keep Richard occupied while the judge walked along behind the row of horses and riders, checking his card.

"Announcing the awards in this class," the announcer said, "Hunters Under Saddle for Riders Seventeen Years of Age and Under. First place goes to number eighty-four. This is Greenwillow, owned by Dr. M. R. Nash and ridden by Laura Sprague. In second place is number thirty-one, Worth Waiting, owned and ridden by Marcy Connolly. In third place is . . ."

Marcy could scarcely keep from whooping as she trotted over to pick up her ribbon, and she emerged from the ring beaming.

"Well done," Sasha said, giving Richard a pat.

"Wasn't he good?" Marcy asked.

"He was, indeed," Sasha said, "and so were you."

Marcy went into the ring for her equitation class still glowing, thinking of the red ribbon Sasha was holding for her. "Come on, Richard," she whispered, "let's do it again."

When the class was over and they were lined up again Marcy waited for the announcement of the awards with her heart fluttering. By the time fourth place was announced she sagged a little, but only on the inside.

She remembered to keep her head up and her back straight. As long as you were in the ring, Sasha had told her, it was important to remember that you were on show and to carry yourself accordingly. Then the announcer called her number for fifth, and she went to pick up the pink ribbon, grinning from ear to ear.

When she got home her parents were in the kitchen. He father was sitting at the kitchen table while her mother bustled around fixing dinner.

"How did it go?" her mother asked.

"Pretty good. See what I got?" Marcy asked, holding the ribbons.

"How nice! Looks like you're getting to be quite a rider."

Marcy blushed. "Well . . ."

"What did you win the ribbons in?"

"This was in Under Saddle, and this was in Eq."

Her mother and father looked so blank that she burst out laughing. Then she tried to explain it to them, realizing that it did sound complicated if you didn't know anything about horse shows. She hoped they wouldn't ask her how she'd done in her jumping classes. They didn't, and she didn't tell them, committing a small sin of omission. Another one was that she didn't mention the fact that Nat had won all three of her jumping classes.

"Those are pretty colors," her father said, "just like a Valentine."

Marcy nodded. "A late Valentine's Day present from Richard. I'm going to hang them on the wall over my bed."

"That will be nice," her mother said. "Now, why don't you go wash? Dinner's almost ready. Hungry?"

"Hungry? I'm *starved.*"

When they sat down to eat her mother said, "Oh, by the way, Marcy, Gene stopped by."

Marcy's fork stopped in midair. Jean? Gene? "Who?"

"Don't get smarty. Gene Thurston. Your piano teacher. Remember him?"

"Oh yeah. What did he want?"

"He dropped off some music and a notice about an audition for Bay Area Young Musicians. It's a new competition that the Symphony Association is sponsoring. Their idea is that young performers work in obscurity for years without getting the kind of exposure and experience they will need for their future careers. So it's for young performers, fourteen and under, and the repertoire is not difficult. Let's see . . ." Her mother jumped up from the table and went out to the front hall. When she came back she had a sheaf of paper in her hand. "Here, look. Why, you played that Mozart three years ago . . ." She went rattling on about the pieces that would be required and what a fabulous opportunity it was.

Marcy's heart sank. Why did her life have to be so up and down? She'd just spent one of the most interesting days of her entire life and her mother didn't even want to hear about it. Instead she was talking on and on about this audition, which was the last thing in the world Marcy wanted to hear about. Whatever her future career was, she was positive it wouldn't have anything to do with the piano.

"Gene says you'll be a shoo-in," her mother went on, "but it would be a good idea to have two lessons a week instead of one. The competition is June twentieth. That's only three months away."

"Two lessons a week!" Marcy spluttered. "I don't even have time for one. Or to practice either."

Her mother shifted in her chair. "I've noticed," she said, with an edge in her voice. "Ever since you met Nat . . . Ever since you got Richard . . ." Then her tone changed abruptly, back to excitement. "It's such a good opportunity. And the first prize is one thousand dollars and a chance to study with Delorosa. He's coming out here for the summer; they've made a special arrangement with Juilliard. Just think of it, Francisco Delorosa! I remember hearing him play a concert at the old Opera House—remember Charles?—one piano all by itself in the middle of the stage. Stark. Then he appeared at stage left, walked slowly across the stage—he had polio as a child, you know, but it only affected his legs, thank heavens, because when he reached the piano and began to play, starkness went right out of the world. It was the Promised Land right there, flowing from his fingers. Just think of it, Marcy, you could actually study with Delorosa!"

"I don't want to study with Delorosa," Marcy said. "And I don't have time for two lessons a week, and I'm not going to play in that audition and—" She paused and took a deep breath, might as well get it all out, "I don't want to play the piano anymore, period."

Her mother dropped her fork and stared at Marcy. "What did you say?"

"I said I don't want to play the piano anymore," Marcy repeated, in a small voice this time.

There was a long moment of silence and Marcy steeled herself for the anger she knew was coming next. Her mother didn't get mad, though. She waved her hand in dismissal. "That's the silliest thing I ever heard," she said. "Don't you agree, Charles?"

"Yes, darling," he said, and Marcy's heart sank to the floor. Whenever her parents banded together, she knew she didn't have a chance. And she'd thought that he would be on her side! "What would you want to quit the piano for?" he asked. "I think it's wonderful."

"Well, I don't. I don't like playing the piano. I'm no good anyway, and I'd rather be riding. I don't have time to do both, with homework and everything. I'm getting exhausted."

It went on like that for the rest of the meal. Marcy tried every argument she could think of, and none of them worked. They didn't change; she didn't change. Finally dinner was over and Marcy went up to her room.

She flopped down on her bed, plotting ways to divorce the piano from her life. Well, she could break her wrist. No way she could play the piano with a broken wrist. But she wouldn't be able to ride, then, either; and how could she just go out and break her wrist? Nope, there had to be a simpler solution.

She turned over on her stomach, thinking hard, but all she could hear were the voices of her mom and dad telling her that it was important for her to continue with her music. If they thought it was so important, why didn't *they* play the piano? Why did they have to make her do it? And then the last thing her mother had said, "Spending hours and hours glued to the piano is not such a horrible fate. Dana's spent hours and hours in the dance studio, and look where it got her."

She *would* bring that up. When Marcy said, "I'm not Dana! And I don't want to be as narrow as she is," her mother got the blank look, the I-know-you-didn't-mean-that-so-I'll-pretend-I-didn't-hear look.

Marcy flopped back onto her back, crossed her legs and stared at the ceiling. She was tired and she had homework to do, but her mind was all jangly. She wished her life could be smooth and peaceful. Just this one day had had enough ups and downs in it to make a person seasick. Just when everything seemed to be working out, going a little bit up for once, making up with Nat and ending up at the show with two pretty good ribbons, boom, her mother hit her with this big down.

". . . I don't know what to do about her."

Marcy sat up and strained to hear her mother's voice as it came drifting up the stairs. She couldn't hear every word, just random phrases, but she knew they were talking about her. She got out of bed and walked to the door, leaving it open in case she had to beat a hasty retreat. Creeping down the stairs, she avoided the third and eleventh steps, which creaked, and sat down on the fifth stair from the bottom. From this position, she knew from experience, she could not be seen, but she could hear what was being said in the dining room.

"Well, darling, she does have a point, you know," came her father's voice.

Prickles raced down Marcy's spine. Was he her ally, after all?

"But I thought you agreed with me!"

"Because we agreed not to disagree in front of the children. Remember?"

"Yes, of course, but, well, I believed you," her mother said with something like despair in her voice.

"Why would it be so awful if she quit? It's obvious that she'd rather ride. And she has been looking tired lately. I've been worried about her."

"Oh, horses, Charles. What's the future in that?"

"Maybe there isn't one. Maybe it's something she'll do for a few years and leave behind. But so what? I think it's great that she wants to experiment and try new things. That's what childhood is for."

There was a long silence, and Marcy held her breath, wanting to get up and cheer, say, "Yes, Daddy, yes, yes, *yes!*"

"I don't think we should encourage her to quit. It worries me the way she's always quitting things."

"She's not quitting riding. Not even talking about it."

"Well"—her mother sighed—"maybe you're right. I'm certainly tired of trying to get her to practice."

"I don't think it's possible to do anything unless you want to. Desire has to be there. And she clearly doesn't have her heart in the piano."

"Understatement of the year. Dana—"

"Tess," he said in the patient voice he used when he was explaining a math problem to Marcy for the third time and she still didn't understand it, "it's not fair to compare them. Dana is unusual. It's rare for someone so young to have that kind of dedication and single-mindedness. Why, when I was Marcy's age I didn't have the slightest idea what I wanted to do—except get off of that farm."

"I still wish she wouldn't give up music."

"So do I, but we can't make that decision for her. It's her life. She might come back to it, and even if she doesn't, she's still been enriched by it."

Marcy grinned and crept back up the stairs, wanting to skip and whoop and holler: She didn't have to play the piano any more! She sank into bed happy that the day had ended on an up, after all. The last things she saw before she went to sleep were the two ribbons hanging over her bed. Now she wouldn't have to rush so in the afternoons, trying to fit in riding and practicing. She could spend more time with Richard. She would work hard, and at the next show . . .

Chapter 18

MARCY HAD NOT realized how much the piano had felt like an albatross. Now that she was free of it she felt lighthearted and luxuriated in the long afternoons she could spend with Richard. Once or twice a week she took advantage of the extra time to take Richard on a long trail ride. It kept the horses from getting sour with too much ring work, and Marcy and Nat loved it too. They rode all through the water district, on narrow trails winding through the woods, up and out onto the open rolling hills. The hills were carpeted with green, and wildflowers grew everywhere, as if they had been in hiding for a year, unable to bloom because of the

drought; but now, since the winter rains, they burst
forth in wild abandon, dotting the hillsides with patches
of mustard yellow and sprinkles of scarlet and purple.
When they came to a gully or a fallen tree Marcy and
Nat grinned with delight because it was something to
jump. They jumped the gullies and fallen trees and low-
growing bushes, intoxicated with the freedom of jumping something that wasn't painted and measured and
enclosed in a ring. The horses would get excited too and
jumped with more boldness and enthusiasm than they
did in the ring at home.

A deep, steady joy glowed all the way through
Marcy, and she thought she could ride like that forever,
with the sky stretching above her, the wind riffling her
hair, and Richard moving powerfully beneath her.

Back at the barn, when their work was done and
the sun was slanting down in the west, she and Nat would
sit on the tack trunk listening to the birds chirping and
the horses chewing their hay. Sometimes they talked;
sometimes they sang; sometimes they simply sat with
their arms draped around each other's shoulders, each
in her own reverie.

If the fog rolled in, it was too cold to sit outside
and they would go up to the house. But they preferred
the barn. It was their territory, and Sasha and Jim never
came out there in the evening. Marcy had to admit that
things were different at Nat's house since Jim had been
around. Two grown-ups filled up the house in a way that
one had not.

One evening in May when they were sitting at the barn as usual, Marcy asked, "Do you think they'll ever get married?"

"Naw. Sasha says that marriage is obsolete. Anyway, you don't have to be married to have a serious, committed relationship."

"I don't think marriage is obsolete. My parents are married."

Nat shrugged. "So were mine, but it's a terribly old-fashioned thing to do."

Were her parents old-fashioned, Marcy wondered, or was it just that Sasha was a Bohemian? "Most people get married," she said, "unless they're Bohemians or something weird like that."

"You can do it if you want, but not me," Nat said. "I'm going to be like my mother, except I'm *never* going to get married: 'Love many, trust few, paddle your own canoe'—that's what I'm going to do."

"I still think it would be nice if they got married. Then Jim would be your stepfather."

"What do I need a stepfather for? I'm going to see my real father as soon as school's out. That's only three more weeks—oh!, I *can't wait!*" Nat exclaimed and she drummed her heels against the trunk in excitement.

Once again the image came back to Marcy: Nat and the handsome blond man on a boat, far across the Pacific, bounding through the waves. She grimaced, feeling left out as she always did when Nat talked about the summer.

"Don't take it so personally," Nat said.

"How else am I supposed to take it?"

"Well, you could think about me, for a change. Don't you know how important this is to me?"

Marcy scuffed at the ground with her toe. "Hadn't thought about that," she mumbled.

Neither of them spoke for a few minutes, and the silence between them was filled with the small sounds of evening—the faint swish of car tires on the street, the wind rustling in the trees, the mournful haunting cry of the doves.

"Anyway," Nat said, putting her arm around Marcy's shoulders, "it's just for the summer. I'll come back."

"Yeah," Marcy said, "after all, we're true friends."

"Um-hm."

After a while they said good night. Nat headed down the path, and Marcy watched her go, a slender ghostly figure with hair painted silver by the moon, drifting away beneath the trees. The dove called again and Marcy felt as mournful as it sounded.

Marcy walked slowly down to Richard's stall. He was lying down, with his legs tucked under him. When she appeared he raised his head and flicked his ears. "You don't know how lucky you are," she said. "If your best friend left, you wouldn't care, would you?"

She waited for an answer, but Richard just blinked sleepily at her. "No," Marcy answered for him. "You wouldn't even know it." She told him good night and headed for her house, thinking how much easier it would be if she were a horse.

ON THE DAYS they didn't go trail riding, they worked in the ring. Now Marcy could ride without stirrups indefinitely and her legs felt firm and steady. She could get Richard on the bit in the space of a circle, and she was making steady progress in jumping, learning more and more about the intricacies of doing a smooth, polished round.

Since the first schooling show they'd been to three more, and Marcy had improved at every one. She'd won ribbons at those shows too, on the flat and over fences. The string of ribbons over her bed was growing.

One afternoon in May, Marcy and Nat went up to Nat's house after they'd ridden and finished their stable chores. On the kitchen counter Sasha had left a note and the prize list for the Santa Rosa Spring Classic Horse Show.

"Oh, hot!" Nat said, "here it is, at last."

They sat down at the kitchen table and thumbed through the prize list, which listed all the classes in the show, named the judges and other officials. Sasha had marked the classes she thought they should enter, so they got pens and filled out the entry blanks. As Marcy wrote she tingled with excitement. It was a big show, a recognized show, and she was going to go! On the way home she made a detour to mail the entries. When she dropped the envelope in the mailbox she felt as if she'd

done something irrevocable, something she would remember for the rest of her life.

She ran the rest of the way home, clomped up the
stairs and flung open the door of her closet. There they
were, hanging on their hangers, in a separate space she'd
made: her show clothes. Pretending that she was getting
ready for the show, she braided her hair and pinned it
on top of her head. Then she put a hairnet over it and
put her hat on, catching any wispy strays of hair with
bobby pins. Next came the shirt, breeches, coat, boots,
and, as a final touch, gloves.

In her parents' bathroom she surveyed herself in
their full-length mirror. The mirror was on the door and
if she turned the door at an angle she could see her back
in the wall mirror, and in that she could see her front,
and in that her back . . . Where did they end, these im-
ages of herself? Or was there an end? They seemed to
go on forever, more reflections that she could count. For
that matter, where did they begin? Was the one facing
her the beginning? The one behind her?

There she was, looking neat and solemn, her eyes
dark under the bill of her hunt cap, boots gleaming,
coat trim. She turned sideways and looked at herself
from that angle—left side, right side, left side, right
side. Marcy straightened her shoulders and felt that she
was dressed exactly right. Nothing she had ever worn
before felt like that. It was as if she had been waiting all
her life, looking for the right thing to wear, the right
person to be, rejecting one image after another, always
somehow dissatisfied, until that moment when it all went

"click," like a kaleidoscope, myriad pieces falling this way and that, capable of hundreds, maybe thousands, of combinations, all of them acceptable, but only one that would be outstanding, that was the one. Click. All the pieces fell into place: the black boots, the navy coat, the tan breeches, the pin-striped shirt, the black velvet hunt cap. And inside was a person who knew where she belonged, what she wanted to do, how she wanted to be. Marcy Connolly, *equestrienne extraordinaire*: a name flashing like a meteor in the horse show world. Soon everyone would take notice when she came into the ring, and even Nat would wish that she was in some other division.

"Watch out, Santa Rosa," she said, "here I come!"

Chapter 19

MARCY'S NAVY COAT and Nat's green one were hanging up behind them in the cab of the truck. Their suitcases were in the back along with the things they would need for the horses at the show—wheelbarrow and hose, saddle racks, tack trunk, feed, tack, blankets. It seemed like a lot of stuff for a four-day show, but they would need it all. They turned into the fairgrounds and stopped at the bulletin board to find out where their stalls were.

"Oh, isn't this exciting?" Marcy asked, looking around eagerly. All around them were the sounds of pounding and hammering as people worked setting up tack rooms and grooming stalls and getting their horses settled in. In the barn aisles big six- and eight-horse vans were pulled up to unload. Haphazard piles of wraps and blankets, saddle racks and boot bags littered the aisles where people had already arrived. Horses just off the vans stood with heads high while grooms bent to unwrap their legs, and horses already in their stalls hung their heads out of the doors whinnying at the new arrivals. Everywhere people were busy—tacking up or untacking, washing horses, unloading trucks. Mothers came wandering down from the office with numbers and programs, little brothers careered down the aisles on bicycles.

"This reminds me of a carnival," Marcy said.

"Apt analogy," Sasha said. "Some of these people live like carnival people too—living in motor homes, on the road for months at a time, moving from one show to the next."

"Look," Marcy said, "it says Portland on that van. Portland, *Oregon*?"

"Yes," Sasha said.

"But that's so far. Why would they come here?"

"It's a big show. People come from all over. This barn is from Malibu, that's almost as far as Portland," Sasha said, nodding her head at the barn nearest them. Two grooms in Levi's and running shoes were covering a stall being used as a tack room with green and white curtains, while another adjusted an oval brass sign that said: Fair Hill Farm, Merl Ellis, Trainer. Down the aisle green-and-white tack trunks were placed neatly in front of each stall.

Nat whistled. "Pretty fancy."

"Oh help," Marcy gulped, her excitement and confidence draining away with a rush. "I'm not ready for this."

"Sure you are," Sasha said. "These other people are no different from you. Everyone does the same thing."

"Yeah, but I'll bet everyone else has done it longer and better than me."

"Not everyone. And how are you going to get experience if you don't do it?"

"I'd rather go to a schooling show," Marcy said. "*Those* were fun."

"Can't stay in the bush leagues forever. This will be fun too. It's just the same as a schooling show except the courses and the judges will be better."

"Yeah, and the *riders*. And the horses. And—"

"Marce, calm down. You're ready for this, believe me."

"Hey, Sharon!" Nat called to a small girl with delicate features who was leading a blood-bay mare. Her red hair was the same color as her horse. "What's up?"

"Nothing much," she said. "How've you been?"

"Great. You?"

"Good. Tell you about it later."

"Who was that?" Sasha asked.

"Sharon Oates. You know her. She won the Medal at Santa Barbara. I changed horses with her in the work-off, remember?"

"Oh, yeah, she rides with Pat Johnson, right?"

"Right."

"Nice mare," Sasha said.

"Um-hm. Thelma's great," Nat said. "Really bold and athletic, but sort of dainty too. Just like Sharon. She looks like a Dresden doll, but she's tough. Tough competitor too."

AFTER THEY'D UNLOADED the horses and the truck, Marcy and Nat tacked up Richard and Joey and rode over to the ring. At the entrance to the ring was a large arched sign that said: Chris Beck Arena. Everyone called it the Beck. It was a large outdoor ring with grandstands on one side and a schooling area on the other. Past the schooling area were green fields and, beyond them, a fringe of mountains, purplish in the distance. In the Beck and the schooling area were dozens of horses, all sizes and colors. The riders were just as motley, outfitted in jeans and chaps and a colorful array of T-shirts and hats.

"Well, here goes," Nat said. She gathered up her reins and started around the ring at a trot. Marcy set off after her, but there was so much going on she couldn't concentrate. In the middle of the ring three jumps were set up and people were jumping them from both directions, ending up in a melee at either end of the ring, which the people working on the rail had to get through as best they could. Riding in that ring was like playing In and Out the Window without any rules. Marcy had to thread her way through the horses walking on the rail, while others cantered up behind her, and others came straight at her from the opposite direction.

It was just as she had feared. Everyone seemed so experienced, so professional, so unfazed by all the commotion—like that blond girl on the black horse. She was part of a group of six or seven whose trainer was a big man with a moustache standing by the schooling fences in the middle of the ring. A shock of black hair fell across his face, and around his neck he wore several gold and silver chains that caught the sun, sending off glittering darts of light.

Nat rode up behind Marcy. "That's Merl Ellis," she said. "He had four riders in the Medal finals last year."

"Hot stuff?" Marcy asked.

"You got it," Nat said.

Marcy's eyes drifted back to the blond girl on the black horse. She came into every jump looking cool and confident and jumped it in perfect form. Although Merl yelled a lot at his other riders, all he ever said to her was, "Good, Delia," or "Okay."

Marcy gathered up her reins and sent Richard into the trot. She'd trotted a few times around the ring when he came to a sudden halt and Marcy pitched forward onto the pommel, jarred by the unexpectedness of it.

"Watch where you're going, will you?"

"Sorry," Marcy mumbled, looking at a slender girl on a blood-bay horse. Her red hair was tied back in a pony tail.

"There are other people here besides you, you you know," she said. "Where'd you come from, anyway?"

"I . . ." Marcy gulped. She didn't see why the girl had to be so rude. She had run into Marcy just as much as Marcy had run into her. "Sorry," she said lamely.

"Well, watch where you're going next time," the red-haired girl said. Then she dug her spur into the horse's side and cantered off. Something about this pair seemed familiar. Marcy watched them canter around the ring and jump the oxer in superb form. Beneath their surface beauty was an expertise that showed clearly in the way they jumped, then cantered around to approach the jump again, as if they were all alone in the ring, in complete command. Marcy snapped her fingers. "Sharon Oates," she mumbled to herself. Nat had greeted her enthusiastically, as if she liked her. Marcy wondered how she could like anyone so rude.

She settled back into the saddle, determined to get to work and stop watching everyone else. She crossed her stirrups over the pommel of the saddle and set Richard back into a trot, trying to get him into a frame with his hindquarters underneath him. She wanted to do some circles and half-turns, but there were so many people she didn't dare try it again. One near crash was enough.

After about twenty minutes she saw Sasha down at the far end of the ring looking somehow trim and clean in the midst of all the dust and mud—dust where the water truck hadn't been, mud where it had. In a few minutes she walked over to the crossbar and Marcy and Nat started trotting back and forth over it, waiting their turn to jump in a line of six or seven other people. Their trainers stood beside the crossbar too, yelling instructions or comments as their students approached the jump and cantered off. After they had trotted the crossbar several times, Sasha made it into a little vertical. They trotted the vertical, then cantered it a few times. Then they went on to canter the bigger vertical and the oxer. Marcy started out stiff and anxious, but Richard was steady and seemed to be bothered neither by her tenseness nor the chaos around him.

"Okay, Marcy," Sasha said finally, "that's enough. I want to do a few more fences with Nat. Why don't you take Richard down to the covered ring and walk him? Your classes tomorrow are in there and you should let him have a look at it."

Marcy left the ring, glad to be out of the crowd. Outside the ring she stopped and watched as Nat jumped over the oxer, which was now about three feet wide and almost four feet high. Her braid flapped gaily as Joey sailed over the fence. Marcy shook her head and smiled, wishing that she had started riding when she was eight, like Nat had. At this show Marcy was entered in Maiden and Novice classes. It was nice to have "easy" divisions like that, since she was just starting out, but she wanted to be good enough to ride in the open junior division and medal classes, like Nat did. She'd get there, Sasha said, but she had to walk before she could run.

The covered ring was not crowded and the gloom inside was cool and welcome after the glare of the Beck. The first time around Richard spooked at a big orange garbage can in the far corner, but Marcy let him look at it and told him it was okay. The next time around he walked right by it. Around and around she walked, humming to herself, enjoying the easy swing of Richard's walk and the smells of horse and sweat and leather. A shiver went down her spine when she realized that the next day she and Richard would be in this ring again. Only this time there would be jumps and a judge and a grandstand full of people watching.

That evening Marcy lay in bed next to Nat, her stomach churning like a cement-mixer. They had to get up before dawn so they would have time to feed and braid and be ready for the first class at seven-thirty, but here it was ten o'clock and she'd never been wider awake in her life. Again she went over what she was going to put on in the morning—shirt and breeches and boots and over that her overalls to keep her breeches and boots clean while she was doing her stable work. She had laid her clothes out on a chair before she went to bed and checked them over twice. Now she checked them over again in her mind.

She lay still and listened to Nat's deep, even breathing, wishing that she would fall asleep too. But the harder she tried to go to sleep, the more wakeful she felt. Scenes from the day kept flashing through her mind, and when she shut her eyes a course appeared. She was trying to remember all the things she was supposed to do—get the right pace and keep it, go deep into her corners, look ahead, check her leads, keep her heels down, find good spots—the list was practically endless, and it was hard to think of so many things at once, never mind *do* them.

Whenever she started to drift off something would jerk her back to consciousness—cars' headlights shining in the window, the slam of a door down the hall, the *thrum, thrum, thrum* of the rock band playing in the lounge. She tossed and turned, then lay on her back and tried putting herself to sleep with a form of self-hypnosis that Old Ronzo had taught them. Once she'd put all the parts of her body to sleep, up as far as her stomach, and was in that drifting place between waking and sleeping where everything felt floaty, when she heard voices outside the door, then the key in the lock. A shaft of light beamed across the floor as Sasha came into the room. She'd been down in the lounge with some of her friends. She went into the bathroom and banged around, making much more noise than she would have if she hadn't been trying to be quiet.

Then the light went off in the bathroom and Marcy could hear her padding slowly across the floor, feeling her way to the other bed. She banged against the chair with Marcy's clothes on it and swore softly under her breath. Marcy had a nearly uncontrollable urge to laugh, which she managed to stifle; she didn't want Sasha to think that she had woken her up. Instead she lay still, pretending to be asleep—while her mind raced with anticipation of the next day.

Chapter 20

BRRNG! BRRNG! MARCY'S eyes flew open, and she groped for the alarm. Running, she'd been running, looking for something. Something she must do—fast. She had to get up to the ring. It was time for her class and she was already late, she . . . The room came into focus and she realized she'd been dreaming, but the urgent feeling was still with her. She jumped out of bed and bustled around the room mumbling her lists to herself as she gathered her things together.

"Calm down, Marce," Nat said, her voice fuzzy with sleep.

"The show," Marcy said, "let's go."

"It's only five-thirty. There's plenty of time. We'd look pretty silly arriving at the show in our nightgowns."

"So get dressed. You know it takes me forever to braid," Marcy said as she pulled on her boots. "I'll wait for you at the truck," she finished as she stepped out the door, ignoring the fact that Nat wasn't dressed and Sasha was still in the bathroom. She was too nervous to sit in the room and watch them move around in a leisurely fashion as if it were any old day.

The truck was locked. It was cold and foggy and Marcy jumped up and down to keep warm. She thought of all the things she had to do at the barn and the panic feeling of the dream welled up in her again. All spring she'd been having a recurrent dream: She was at a show and her class was being called, but she wasn't ready—couldn't find her boots or saddle or some other essential thing. Last night was the worst one of all. The paddock manager's voice cracked through the barn area: "Okay, you twelve to thirteen year olds, listen up! We need horses up here. Time to check in. Check in, *please!*" Marcy grabbed her tack and ran down to Richard's stall. Inside was clean straw banked just like she'd left it, a flake of hay in the corner and the water bucket hanging on a hook. But no horse. *Where was Richard?* She ran off down the aisle, turned the corner and raced up the next aisle. No Richard. "Richard!" she called. "Have you seen my horse?" she asked the people in the aisle. They shook their heads and she ran on, up one aisle and down another. The voice pursued her, "Listen up you twelve to thirteen year olds! We need horses up here. Time ..."

Marcy wiped the sweat beading on her forehead despite the fog and the cold. Calm down she told herself, it was just a dream. I know exactly where he is. Barn B, third stall from the end. I know where he is and I've got everything I need. It'll be all right, if I ever get there. She jumped up and down again, from nervousness as much as cold. What were Nat and Sasha doing? She was halfway up the stairs to their room when they appeared. At last.

When they arrived at the fairgrounds it was still dark. Most of the barns were still shut up for the night, but here and there a light shone in a stall where a braider worked, standing on a stepladder, her fingers flying through the horse's mane.

Their headlights picked up a groom with a longe whip in her hand leading a horse along the road toward the ring.

"I'm sure glad Richard doesn't have to be longed," Marcy said.

"Oh, shut up," Nat said, because she did have to longe Joey. He needed to buck and play on the longe for ten or fifteen minutes. Otherwise he'd be too fresh and would get strong in the ring. Richard was so relaxed he didn't need it.

While they were feeding and watering, Sasha left to get them some breakfast. Nat went off to longe Joey, and Marcy set to work on Richard.

By seven-thirty she was finished. Richard's coat was glossy and clean and his mane was braided in thirty-six neat braids, tied with navy blue yarn to match her coat. "Pretty good, if I say so myself," she mumbled. "You'll do," she told Richard, giving him a pat. Then she went to the tack room to get herself ready.

She peered at herself in the mirror and her eyes looked back at her anxiously. Calm down, she told her reflection, you've done this before. Besides, you look pretty good, you know. Now all you've got to do is go out there and *do* good. Simple. "Yah, simple," she said out loud, fighting down a wave of panic. When she was finished dressing she patted her hair for about the tenth time, then took her number off the wall and tied it around her waist: 542. It didn't seem like a lucky number, but it didn't seem like an unlucky one either. It would be nice to have a real lucky number like 333, but 542 seemed okay. At least it wasn't 13.

By the time she was on and heading up to the ring it was full light and there were only a few wisps of fog lingering along the road. When she got up to the ring she went over to the announcer's stand to look at the course. A knot of people, some on foot, some on horseback, were gathered there and Marcy craned her neck to see the course through the crowd. The green wood of the announcer's stand was peppered with varicolored triangular bits of paper stuck to it with staples where courses had been posted in the past, but there was no course up for today. She looked into the ring at the jumps, trying to figure out what the course might be. The ring had been dragged and the jumps were all in position. They were brightly colored and flanked with flowers. The lights were on, and instead of yesterday's aura of peaceful gloom, there was a bright expectant hush like a stage set just after the curtain goes up.

She turned to a girl standing next to her who was also looking somewhat vaguely into the ring. "Do you know the course?" she asked.

The girl shook her head. "No," she said, "it's not posted."

"Are you in the first class? Maiden Equitation Over Fences?"

The girl nodded. "You?"

Marcy nodded.

"Well, the course is supposed to be posted one hour before the class. That's a rule. Merl is really mad. And this is supposed to be a recognized show!"

"Merl?"

"Yeah," the other said impatiently. "Merl Ellis, my trainer." Her voice had an edge of sarcasm to it, as if any idiot would know who Merl Ellis was.

Then it came back to Marcy, and her heart sank. The girl she was talking to was the blond girl she'd noticed the day before at the Beck. The one called Delia. The one on the black horse who jumped every fence perfectly. She sure didn't ride like someone in Maiden. If the other people in this class were that good, Marcy wouldn't have a chance. She gave the jumps a last grim look and walked across the road to the schooling ring. It was teeming with people and looked just like the Beck had yesterday. Only now, instead of chaps and T-shirts with hair flying all over the place, all the riders looked neat and elegant in their show clothes, and their horses were immaculate.

When Sasha arrived she asked Marcy if she knew the course.

"No," Marcy said, "when I came up it wasn't posted."

"Okay, I'll go take a look. Are you ready to jump?"

"Yes," Marcy said, trying to ignore a little surge of panic rising inside her. Instead she concentrated on Richard as she threaded her way among the other horses and riders.

When Sasha came back, Marcy settled into the familar warm-up routine: trot the X, canter the vertical and the oxer. She almost forgot that this was her first big show. She almost forgot that in a very few minutes she would no longer be just one more person in the mass of riders warming up. She would be in the ring, under the lights, all alone.

When she was finished warming up the class had started. She followed Sasha across the road to the ring and stood at the end, near the in-gate. "I'll tell you the course," Sasha said, "then you watch a few rounds to get a sense of how it rides. I put your number in. You go in ten."

Marcy nodded, her mouth so dry she couldn't talk.

Sasha told her the course and concluded, "It's pretty straightforward. Just get a good pace and keep it. And pay attention in your corners."

Marcy nodded again. After she'd watched a few people go she had the course memorized, but she kept going over it several more times so when she was in the ring she wouldn't have to think about it: it would be almost automatic.

"Two twenty-two on deck. Five forty-two, you're in the hole!" he gateman called.

Marcy walked over to the in-gate and stood behind 222. She went into the ring and the gateman called, "Five forty-two?"

"Right here," she said.

"Okay," he said. "You're next."

Marcy waited, stomach churning, heart hammering, willing 222 to take forever. But it didn't take her any longer than it did anyone else, about a minute, then the gate swung open and Marcy was in the ring. Richard's ears swiveled back and forth as he tried to take in everything at once—the crowd in the grandstand, the horse that was just finishing the course, the dogs chasing each other up and down the rail outside the ring. Then his ears would flick back, searching for a clue from Marcy as to what was going to happen next. "Okay, Richard, here goes," she whispered as she gathered up her reins and pressed his side with her right leg. She cantered past the grandstand and circled to the left.

Canter, jump, turn; canter, jump, turn. Around they went, and almost before she knew it, she was heading out the gate, panting, sweating, exhilarated, relieved.

"Pretty good," Sasha said. "A little rough around the edges, but not bad. Not bad at all."

"What could I have done better? I want to be *really* good."

"Well, you were too deep to the gate. And your pace could have been more even. You started out too slow and ended up too fast."

"Yeah, I felt as if he was practically running away coming home. I guess he knows where the gate is."

Sasha laughed. "Sure he does. That's one thing all horses know."

Marcy got off, ran her stirrups up, and loosened the girth. "I'll take him back to the barn now. I don't have another class for a while yet."

"No. You wait until this class is over. You might get a ribbon."

"Really? Even after what you said?"

"Yes, really. I haven't seen any really good goes. Anyway, you should always wait until the class is pinned before you go back to the barn, unless you did something that would disqualify you, like going off course or stopping out or falling off."

"Okay."

"I'm going up to the Beck now. Nat's class should be starting pretty soon."

Marcy watched Sasha's slender figure going up the road to the Beck. She wished she could go up there now too, but if Sasha told her to wait here, she would wait.

After what seemed like forever, the announcer said, "This is your class, judge," and a few minutes later, "Announcing the awards in class number thirty-three, Maiden Equitation Over Fences for riders twelve and thirteen years of age. In first place is one thousand eleven, Delia Duncan, riding Night Moves, second three eighty-two . . ." Marcy held the reins in one hand and scratched Richard's neck with the other as she listened to the announcer. Say "five forty-two," she thought, "five forty-two." But he went through the ribbons, down to sixth place, and did not call her number. The fact that Delia Duncan won was no surprise. Well, at least she wouldn't be in Maiden any more.

Marcy hadn't really expected to get anything, nevertheless a tickle of hope had been flickering inside her. She turned toward the barn and to her surprise felt her throat closing up and tears welling in her eyes. What was she crying for? She'd done the best she could. So, she didn't get a ribbon. So what? Still her shoulders sagged and her feet dragged as she trekked back to the barn. Slightly ahead of her she saw a girl with a white ribbon in her hand. Marcy felt a wave of jealousy. Then she remembered something her father had told her: Even if you don't feel like it, if you smile and say something nice, you'll probably feel better.

She caught up with the other girl, glanced at her casually as they walked along. The girl met her eyes and Marcy smiled.

"Congratulations," she said.

"Oh, thanks," she said, her eyes sparkling. "I'm so excited. That's the first ribbon I've ever won at a recognized show."

Marcy smiled back at her. "That's terrific. Is this your first big show?"

The girl nodded. "How 'bout you?"

"Me too," Marcy said. "I was *so* nervous."

"So was I," said the other girl, "beforehand. But once I was in the ring I had so many things to think about I didn't have time to be nervous."

"Yeah," Marcy said, "the rest of the world just fades away."

By the time they came to the turn-off for the girl's barn, Marcy had found out that her name was Louise Albergini. She was from San Jose and her trainer was Pat Johnson. Her horse was named Willie and she'd owned him for a year and a half.

"If you ride with Pat Johnson then you must know Sharon Oates," Marcy said.

"Sure, I know her."

"She's kind of stuck-up, isn't she? Yesterday in the Beck she ran into me. Then she accused *me* of running into *her*. Acted like it was my fault."

"Oh, that's just a manner she has. When she's riding she gets intense. But she's really nice. You'll see."

"I guess so," Marcy said, not entirely convinced.

"Well, here's my barn," Louise said. "Are you in the Novice Eq Over too?"

"Yes."

"See you then," Louise said, "in about two hours."

Marcy smiled as she watched Louise turn down the aisle to her barn, and found herself looking forward to the next class when she would meet her again.

"That was just the first class," she told Richard as she put him away, "and we didn't make complete fools out of ourselves, even if we didn't win a ribbon. There will be other classes. And there's always tomorrow. And the day after that. And the *show* after that. At least it's not like dancing, where there's only one crummy recital a year."

Chapter 21

IT WASN'T LIKE dancing, but it was. When the time
came to go "on stage," Marcy waited outside the gate
with the by-now-familiar fluttering in her stomach while
her heart went *thump, thump* against her breastbone.
Then she was in the ring again—alone. No music, no
partner, no corps de ballet. It was her act, and it was
always a solo. Every time, she vowed to make her round
as good as she could. Only something happened: She'd
get deep to this, long to that; Richard would buck in the
corners, miss a lead, knock a rail down. Once, she went
off-course and left the ring with cheeks burning and
shame in her heart. It didn't help much when Sasha told
her that she wasn't the first person in the world to go off-

course. Everyone did it sooner or later. Marcy wondered why it couldn't be later.

No matter what, she waited, hoping, for the end of every class she rode in, to hear the results. More often than not it was Delia Duncan whose number was called first. Marcy was winning ribbons in her flat classes, but had yet to get anything over fences. Nat, on the other hand, had won one hunter class in her age group and the Under Saddle; she won her eq class, she got two seconds with Joey in First Year Green. She won one medal class and was third and fourth in two others. Sharon Oates was doing very well too. By Saturday Sharon and Nat were neck and neck for high point in both divisions of their age group, equitation and hunters.

"Hurry up and wait is the name of the game," Sasha had said on the first day of the show, and now Marcy knew exactly what she meant. At the barn she would hurry up, grooming Richard, getting herself dressed, hustling to get up to the ring in time for her class. That was the hurry-up part. Then came the waiting: waiting for her turn in the ring, waiting for the class to be over, or for her next class to begin. Sometimes the waiting dragged out for hours. Then she and Nat would sit with Louise and Sharon or some of the other people they knew, soaking up the sun in the grandstand, feeling drowsy, watching whatever class was in progress. Louise had been right about Sharon. When she was on her horse she was all business, but when she wasn't riding she was different. She had a dry sense of humor and could be a lot of fun. They'd sit in the grandstand up at the Beck or in the captain's chairs in front of their tack room, cleaning tack, rolling wraps, talking, waiting . . .

Sometimes Marcy would be seized with restlessness. Then she took off by herself and roved through the barn area, listening, observing. Some of the barns, like Fair Hill Farm where Delia Duncan rode, were very fancy, decorated with stall guards in the stable colors and matching trunks beside each stall. No matter how fancy the trappings were, though, the activity at each barn was the same—grooms hustling around in raggedy Levi's and T-shirts with rub rags dangling from their hip pockets, riders heading up to the ring or coming back, people sitting in front of tack rooms eating or talking. There were piles of leg wraps on the ground and blankets draped on stall doors, bridles and martingales dangling from tack hooks. And even if the aisle was watered and raked, at the end of it was the inevitable manure pile topped with balled-up bailing wire and a stray soda pop can or two. No one noticed Marcy as she walked along. She was just another girl dressed in boots and breeches. It pleased her to know that the way she was dressed labeled her as an exhibitor, someone who fit right in.

On these walks to pass time she counted the ribbons hung over tack rooms. By Saturday, the third day of the show, Fair Hill Farm had twenty-two ribbons, fifteen red, ten yellow, five white, one pink and two championships. Pat Johnson's was a bigger barn, and they had a total of one hundred and seven ribbons, more than Fair Hill Farm. After a ribbon-counting trip, Marcy would return to their tack room and survey their ribbons: Nat's four blue ribbons fluttered at the beginning of the string. Marcy's ribbons hung at the end—her string began where the Fair Hill string stopped: a fifth, a seventh and an eighth—all from flat classes.

ON SATURDAY AFTERNOON Marcy was sitting in the grandstand up at the Beck with Nat and Louise and Sharon feeling even drowsier than usual. She was getting progressively more tired as the show wore on; three days of getting up at dawn, doing her morning chores at the barn, then riding and running back and forth to the barn all day were taking their toll. The class they were watching was Open Working Hunters. Marcy yawned. The horses were gorgeous, but it was like counting sheep. They all looked alike. She yawned again and glanced around. The woman sitting on their left was knitting and had a thermos of coffee by her feet. Somebody's mother, no doubt. It was easy to spot mothers. They wore straw hats, carried their purses with them and were a good deal cleaner than anybody else. Some of them even wore skirts. Those were the mothers-who-watched. They spent most of their time sitting in the grandstands. Then there were the mothers-who-worked. They wore Levis's and hiking boots and were distinguishable from the grooms only because they were older. That morning Marcy had seen one mucking out a stall. She couldn't imagine her mother mucking out her stall. But her mother wasn't either sort. She was a mother-who-stayed-home. It was probably just as well: Marcy never could do anything right while her mother was watching.

'Yoo hoo," Nat said, "Earth calling Marcy. Earth calling Marcy."

Marcy shook her head and the scene came back into focus. The Open Working Hunters was over and the ring crew was changing the fences for the next class, the Equitation Classic. It was to be run like a medal class with a work-off among the top four competitors. With Nat and Sharon tied for first in the equitation division, this class, being the last equitation class of the show, would be the deciding factor.

"When do you go?" Nat asked Sharon.

"Twenty-eighth."

"I'm twenty-fifth. Let's watch a few to see how the course rides."

"Okay, and you better watch out, Natasha Jones, I'm feeling on today."

"*You* better watch out," Nat said. "I wouldn't mind being eq champion, and Joey's never felt better."

When the first horse came on course they all shook off their langor and watched attentively. They agreed that the course was difficult, but fair. There were lots of option lines and it would take thoughtful riding and a bold, scopy horse to lay down the kind of smooth-flowing trip that won ribbons in eq classes.

After a few more horses had gone Nat stood up and stretched. "Time for action," she said. "You coming, Marcy?"

"Do you need any help?" Marcy asked.

"No."

"Then I think I'll stay here. I could use a rest."

"Okay, see you in a bit."

They shook hands, first in the regular way, then with one finger curled inside around the other's finger. Then they stepped one pace backwards and held up their hands with their palms facing each other and their fingers straight up, pointing skywards, like St. Demetrius in Nat's icon. This ritual ended with each of them saying "good luck" in Russian. It was a routine they'd adopted for luck whenever one of them was going to ride in a class, and it was already a sort of tradition.

Sharon and Nat clattered down the steps of the grandstand and Marcy and Louise settled back to watch the class. Only the top equitation riders at the show were entered in this class and the quality of the riding was excellent. By the time it was Nat's turn to go, Marcy was more nervous than if she'd been riding herself.

When Nat and Joey came into the ring Marcy sat on the edge of her seat, clenching her hands into fists. The first fence was a big wall, part of a tricky, long two-stride, short three-stride combination. It was one of the big trouble spots. Marcy held her breath as Nat approached the wall. Joey's ears were pricked forward and his head was higher than usual, indicating a certain amount of tension, but Nat looked relaxed and confident. She did the combination nicely. Three fences done seven to go. Her whole body tense, Marcy never took her eyes off them as they negotiated the rest of the course. As they approached each fence she bent her body forward and when they jumped she jerked her knee up, as if it would help them clear the fence. Maybe Marcy's intensity helped, for Nat jumped every fence as well as she had the first three, negotiating the other trouble spots with ease. When she was finished, Marcy and Louise whooped and yelled and stomped their feet up and down, rattling the boards of the grandstand *fortissimo*.

Marcy jumped up, "I'm going down there," she said. "What a terrific trip!"

Louise pulled her back. "It was gorgeous. But stay here. Sharon goes in about two more and you can't see very well from down there."

Marcy settled back into her seat and soon Sharon was in the ring, looking so cool she might have been out for an afternoon hack. "She's really tough," Marcy said.

Louise nodded. "The stiffer the competition, the better she gets. And she's really up for this one."

Sharon was in complete control from the moment she entered the ring and rode a round that couldn't be faulted.

"Whew," Marcy said, "I'm glad I'm not the judge."

"Stand by for the work-off, please," the announcer's voice cut in, and a deep hush settled over the crowd. No one stirred until the announcer said, "Numbers three o one, five forty-three, thirty-eight and ten twenty-one please stand by. You will work off in this order: number three o one, five forty-three, thirty-eight and ten twenty-one."

Over at the schooling ring where the riders were gathered, little whoops went up when each number was called. Marcy and Louise looked at each other and said almost in unison, "Too much!" Three o one was Sharon. Five forty-three was Nat.

The announcer announced the work-off course, then repeated the instructions and called, "Number three o one? You're in!"

And Sharon was in the ring again, looking cool as ever. The work-off course was even more difficult than the course for the first round had been, and Sharon made it look easy. The last line was a combination of three fences down the long side of the ring in front of the grandstand. Marcy and Louise sat riveted as she approached the first fence in the line. She jumped it nicely, but something bright caught Marcy's eye. It was her stirrup, flapping loose, glinting in the sun. You'd never know she'd lost a stirrup by the way she jumped through that line, though. Then she finished up with a circle and left the ring at a sitting trot while the crowd clapped and cheered.

"Nobody's going to beat that!" Louise said.

"But she lost her stirrup through that last line. That's a major fault in an eq class."

"She did? I didn't see it."

Marcy turned in consternation to the woman on her left, "Did you see it?"

The woman nodded, and Marcy turned back to the ring to watch Nat, who had just come on course. From the first fence to the last Nat and Joey flowed around the course, meeting each fence exactly right, bending through the turns, making the difficult course look easy. It was a trip Marcy would remember for a long time. The rest of the crowd was similarly impressed: When Nat went out the gate there was a moment of absolute silence, then pandemonium broke loose. When she was out of the gate Nat threw her arms around Joey, then jumped off and gave Sasha a big hug.

"That's it," Marcy said, "she's got it in the bag."

She and Louise walked out of the grandstand and made their way over to the schooling ring. Sharon and Nat were standing by the in-gate waiting for the announcement of the awards.

The loudspeaker crackled and the announcer said, "How about a round of applause for the exhibitors in this class? It was an exceptionally fine class and we would like to thank all of the participants for their excellent performances . . ." he rattled on, reiterating the class specifications, then talking about the people who had donated the trophy while the tension at the back gate mounted until even the horses felt it. They sidled restively around, pawing at the ground, tossing their heads impatiently. At last the announcer said, "First place and this lovely trophy, donated by Watson's Tack and Feed Shop, go to number three-o-one, Sharon Oates. Sharon is from Los Altos Hills and was riding her own entry, Good Measure. In second place is number five forty-three, Natasha Jones . . ."

Marcy's mouth dropped. "She lost a stirrup!" she said to Sasha. "How could Sharon win? She lost a stirrup."

"Did she?" Sasha asked. "I didn't see it, so I doubt

if the judge did either. He's sitting on this side of the ring."

Sharon and Nat emerged from the ring with their ribbons and Marcy and Louise joined them as they walked back to the barn. Marcy was boiling inside and could hardly keep her mouth shut until Louise and Sharon turned off to go to their barn.

"It's not fair," she burst out, "you should have won."

"How do you figure that? Sharon had a beautiful trip."

"But she lost a stirrup!"

Nat turned from unbuckling Joey's bridle. "No kidding?"

"No kidding."

"Well, I didn't see it and the judge obviously didn't see it either, so what difference does it make?"

Marcy sputtered. "I can't believe it! 'What difference does it make?'" she repeated, mimicking Nat's tone. "Can't you see? It means you should have won and Sharon would have been fourth."

Nat shrugged. "'Should' doesn't have anything to do with it."

"But . . . but . . . aren't you going to do anything about it?"

"Like what? Stage a midnight raid and snatch her ribbon? Go punch her out? What did you have in mind?"

"I don't know, but you must be able to do *something.*"

"Marce, you know the rule: All decisions of the

judge are final. Once the ribbons are announced, that's it."

Just then a voice from the loudspeaker sounded. "Attention in the barn area. Announcing the championships for the equitation division, riders twelve and thirteen years of age. In first place, and champion is number three-o-one, Sharon Oates. The reserve champion is number five forty-three, Natasha Jones. Congratulations, girls! The ribbons are at the office waiting for you, if you would like to come by and pick them up. Announcing the championships . . ." the voice repeated.

Marcy kicked angrily at the ground, "It's not fair! You should have won it. If I were Sharon I would consider that a tainted ribbon. I wouldn't want a ribbon that I knew I didn't deserve."

"Well, you'll get some," Nat said. "If I make a mistake and the judge doesn't see it, then I figure that's the breaks. Today, Sharon got the breaks. It's all part of the ball game. Sometimes you have really good goes and don't get anything. It evens out in the long run."

"Maybe," Marcy said, "but I still say it's not fair. I don't see how you can be so philosophical about it."

"It's just that I know what it's like. It's the real world, not a fairly tale. There aren't any fairy godmothers around here to reward the just and punish the wicked." She handed Joey's lead rope to Marcy and Marcy held it while Nat sponged him off. "Anyway," Nat said, with a determined edge to her voice, "this show isn't over yet. We've got the Hunter Stake tomorrow, and I, for one, think a championship would look nice up there." She paused and glanced up at the string of ribbons fluttering above their tackroom. "Today was Sharon's day, and tomorrow just may be mine."

Chapter 22

ON SUNDAY MORNING Marcy sat with Louise in the grandstand to watch the Junior Hunter Stake. Marcy kept her fingers crossed, hoping that Nat would win. At the same time she hoped that Sharon wouldn't, but she kept this thought to herself. She didn't want Louise to think she was chewing on sour grapes.

As it turned out, though, the whole thing was an anticlimax. Nat had a rail down and Sharon had a refusal—major faults which eliminated any chance for a ribbon. So Dorothy Livermore was champion and Sharon was reserve because she had more points over fences than Nat did. Marcy felt cheated. She'd been looking forward to it as a chance for Nat to redeem herself, to show Sharon.

"Look, Marce," Nat said when the class was over, "this is a horse show, not the showdown at the OK Corral. There are so many variables that in any given class any one of ten or twenty people could win. It's not like running or swimming where you more or less know who the top two or three finishers will be. Besides I don't have any grudge against Sharon, or Dorothy, either."

"But aren't you mad? Don't you *care*?"

"Sure, I care, but what I care about most is Natasha Jones. I have to live with myself and when I do something stupid, then I get mad. So Joey pulled a rail. It wasn't my fault. It was just one of those things."

Later that day Marcy mulled over this conversation as she bustled around the barn getting Richard ready for the Novice Hunter Stake. It was her last class over fences and she was hoping to do well, to get a ribbon, and finish the show on a good note. Maybe when she'd won as many ribbons as Nat had, when she'd been showing as long and had experienced it for herself, she would be that philosophical about it. But for now, she still felt eager.

She gave Richard a finishing swipe with the rub rag, then stepped back to admire her handiwork. The sun was already edging off toward evening but it still picked up the red highlights in his coat, the white of his sock and stripe. Marcy swung on and headed up to the ring. Maybe his sock would make them lucky today. She hoped so. It was her last chance.

She had looked at the course beforehand and when she got to the ring she paused and looked at it again, going over the sequence of fences and turns, getting it firmly imbedded in her mind. No matter what else she did, she was determined not to go off-course again.

As she turned into the schooling ring she smiled, remembering how left out she had felt on the first day. She'd thought that she was the only one who hadn't been doing it forever, the only one who ever made mistakes. Now she knew better. Other people went off-course, added strides, missed leads, stopped, crashed: They were all in it together. By now she knew most of the people in her division and she enjoyed the camaraderie that had developed among them when they met in the warm-up ring, stood by the gate waiting for their turn, or walked back to the barn after the class was over. She called hello to Jennifer and Melissa. Then she found Louise and they hacked around together. Marcy smiled at Delia Duncan too, but she, looking cool and confident as usual, acted as if she didn't even see Marcy.

"What a snob," Marcy said to Louise.

"Yeah, she's got a swelled head if I ever saw one."

"I hope I'm not like that when I get that good," Marcy said. "*If* I get that good."

"Me too," said Louise, "but I just know we're bound for glory. Sooner or later."

"I think it's going to be later," Marcy said. "I sure haven't whacked anybody out at this show."

"You had a great round yesterday," Louise said.

"Only one small problem, though," Marcy said, "it wasn't the right course."

Louise laughed. "Oh well, another day, another class. Let's make this one perfect, okay?"

"Sure," Marcy said, "I'll be perfect and you'll be perfect plus."

She and Louise were trotting around the schooling ring together laughing at this vision of themselves when Sasha appeared.

"Okay, Marce, are you ready?" she called.

"Huh? Oh yeah, I guess so."

"Have you cantered yet?"

"No."

"Did you put your number in?"

"No."

"Well, I guess you're not ready, then, are you?"

"I guess not."

"Well, get going and I'll go put your number up. Then, when I get back, I'll make an X and you can start warming up. Oh, I almost forgot—did you see your parents?"

"Huh?"

"Your parents. You know, your mother, your father. Charles and Tess Connolly."

"No, I didn't know they were coming! They didn't tell me they were coming."

"Well, they're here. They came up with Jim and I saw them just a minute ago over in the grandstand."

Oh no, Marcy thought, I'm nervous enough without

them watching. What did they have to come for? I know I'll mess up if my parents are watching and this is my last chance. And Jim! She didn't want him to see her mess up either.

When Sasha came back she said, "There's eleven in front of you. You'd better get going. Come on down over this." She pointed to the X.

Marcy tried to settle into the routine of warming up, but she was rattled. Her timing was off. When she didn't get left, she was ahead of her horse.

"Okay, Marce, settle down. It's just another fence. Stay over your leg and *wait*," Sasha called as she headed for the fence. "All right, that was better. Do it again, just like that."

Marcy concentrated on Sasha's voice and gradually settled down. She started getting into her fences right and began to feel the rhythm of Richard underneath her, instead of heading for the fence all tensed up, convinced that it wouldn't be right.

"All right," Sasha said at last, "let's go on that."

On the way over to the ring Sasha asked if she knew the striding.

"Yes," Marcy said, "three and three down the first line, six or seven on that bending line, five down the far side, then one and four."

"Right. I want you to pay attention on that bending line. It's a little tricky. Are you going to do it in six or seven?"

"I don't know. I'll just see when I get there."

"You'd better make up your mind now. Have a plan. I want you to *ride* the course. Don't just let it happen."

"Okay, I'll do it in six, then. It's coming home and he shouldn't have any problem."

"Okay, just don't bow out too much and pay attention to that turn at the far end; it's tighter than it looks."

"Okay."

"And have fun."

"Oh, sure. I know I'm going to mess up with my parents here. I can't ever do anything right when my mother is watching. And Jim. He thinks I know how to ride."

Sasha laughed. "And so you do. But he'll think you're doing great if you just get around. So will your mother and father. They don't know enough to know the difference between a good go and a bad one. But *I* do. So think positively and do a good one. It's your last chance."

Sasha walked off toward the grandstand and Marcy went to look at the blackboard by the gate. There were only three horses in front of her. She shortened her reins and turned toward the open space at the end of the ring beyond the gate, walking and trotting back and forth to keep Richard loosened up. At the ends she did leg yields and tight little turns to get his mouth soft and his mind on bending. All the while she was running through the course in her mind.

"Five forty-two?" the gateman called.

"Right here," Marcy said, coming up to the gate. She breathed a little prayer that this time she would ride like Sasha said she could, that she wouldn't make any stupid mistakes like she had yesterday.

"Okay, five forty-two, you're in," the gateman said, as he swung the gate open for her.

Then she was in the ring, cantering her warm-up circle. Not enough pace, she thought, and put a little more leg on Richard. Keep him in a frame, Sasha's voice in her head said. Richard moved forward obediently to her leg and she increased the tension on the reins a little to keep him from getting too strung out. Then they were over the brush and turning left. Leg at the gate, don't want to stall, need impulsion for this line. One, two, three fences, three strides between each one. That seemed okay. Now *lots* of left leg, this is the corner he likes to cut. Good, keep on the rail, keep him together for the bending line. Now, leg, leg, leg, keep him moving, don't bow out too much, this should look like a smooth, easy six. Richard sailed over the last fence on that line. All right. Now keep him together for the far line in five normal. Okay, now right leg for this turn, get straight for the in-and-out. In they jumped, and out, smooth and fluid. Now canter, canter, canter. Keep your rhythm coming home. She felt Richard gathering his hindquarters to jump the last fence, and they were done!

Marcy dropped her reins and patted Richard on the neck, came out of the ring feeling good. It was the best round she'd ever done.

Sasha met her at the back gate, looking pleased. "Nothing wrong with that go," she said. "That was really good."

"Yeah," Nat said, "it was *great!*"

"You think I'm beginning to get it together?" Marcy asked, beaming.

"Definitely," Sasha and Nat said nearly in unison.

"So can I go three feet six at the next show?"

"You could," Sasha said. "You're capable of it, but a couple more shows at three feet might be a good idea. There's no big rush. But don't collapse on his neck like that after the last fence."

Marcy hopped off Richard and handed the reins to Nat who held them while Marcy ran up the stirrups and loosened the girth. "I was just patting him. I wanted him to know how good he was."

"That's nice," Sasha said, "but a round begins when you come in the gate and ends when you go out of it. A neat finish is just as important as everything else."

"Okay, no patting until I'm outside the gate."

"Good," Sasha said, smiling at her. "You can pat him all you want once you're outside the ring."

Now Marcy's parents and Jim emerged from the crowd milling around by the back gate.

"How 'bout a hug?" her father asked. "You were terrific, Marshmallow."

"One for me too," Jim said.

Marcy hugged them, then turned to her mother.

"You looked *wonderful,*" her mother said.

"As good as Dana?"

"Well, it's hard to compare dancing and riding—they're different—but you were performing, with lots of people watching you. You didn't panic and you looked so grown-up and businesslike, I thought you were terrific."

"You sure were," her father said. "I bet you won it."

"Oh, I don't think so. I'll be happy if I get anything. And even if I don't, I know that I did the best I could."

"And you managed Richard with lots of aplomb. That's quite an accomplishment," her mother added, glancing at Richard with a trace of apprehension. "Big strong horse like that."

"She's getting to be quite a rider," Sasha said.

"You've been wonderful to Marcy," her father said. "How can we ever thank you?"

"No need. I enjoy it and having a student like Marcy is all any teacher could ask for."

"Thanks a lot," Nat said.

Sasha turned to Nat. "Well, you're in a different category: daughter."

"I'm your student too."

"This is true. And a good one." Sasha put an arm around each of them. "Having two students like you is all any teacher could ask for," she amended. "How's that, Natasha?"

Nat ducked her head in acknowledgment.

Marcy's mother reached for Sasha's hand and shook it. "I must admit that I was less than enthusiastic when

Marcy first developed this passion for riding. But . . . well . . ." She paused and ran her hand through her hair. "Marcy's a different person since you and Nat moved in, and we're grateful."

Marcy scratched Richard's neck while she studied the scene. When her mother first started talking, Sasha looked surprised. Then her face broke out in her special warm smile. "Well, thank you," she said. "It's been a pleasure for me. Riding's a challenge. You have to have your emotions in control, and your body too. Marcy's made a lot of progress in a short time. She's got a lot of ability, and above all, she's got perseverence and she's not afraid to work. That's the most important thing."

"I agree," her mother said, slipping her arm around Marcy's shoulder and giving her a squeeze. "We sure are proud of you, Marce."

Nat rolled her eyes and mouthed "mushy" at Marcy, but Marcy was savoring every word.

"Now you can relax," Jim said. "Come sit with us?" he asked, offering Marcy his arm as if they were at a grand ball.

Marcy giggled. She loved it when Jim treated her like that. "I can't now. I have to wait for the end of this class. If I get a ribbon I have to trot Richard into the ring, so the judge can check him for soundness."

"Later then?"

Marcy nodded, smiling at them all as they turned to go sit back down in the grandstand. As she watched the little group heading toward the grandstand, picking their way through the horses milling around by the gate, she had to smile to herself. Sasha and Nat moved confidently, but her parents and Jim made wide berths of the horses and looked at them suspiciously, as if at any minute they might do something alarming.

Now came the waiting part of the hurry up and wait. Marcy hooked her arm through the reins and hung onto the rail with her hands while she watched some horses go. Over in the grandstand she could see her mother sitting next to Sasha, talking, looking happy and relaxed. Maybe she was learning what the judge was looking for. Maybe she'd decided that even if Sasha was a Bohemian, she was a nice person too. After all, if it wasn't for her, Marcy wouldn't be there at all. Her mother wouldn't have said, "We sure are proud of you." Her mother caught her eye, waved and smiled. Marcy felt good all over again and thought how nice it was to have a mother-who-watched, after all.

Then it was Louise's turn in the ring. She had a nice trip and when she came out the gate Marcy called, "Good-o!" After Louise talked to Pat about her round she came over to join Marcy and they stood together, watching the horses come and go in the ring.

"This is your class, judge," the announcer said at last, and the characteristic silence descended on the people gathered around the back gate, waiting for the end of the class. The runner took the judge's card and came down to the announcer's stand: "Announcing the awards in class number one forty-three, Novice Working Hunter Stake for riders seventeen and under," the announcer said. "In first place is one o one, second, five forty-two, third, thirty-four, then one thousand eleven, twenty-six, five o eight, three ninety-eight, and two o four. Will you trot in in that order, please. Number one o one . . ."

As in a dream Marcy floated through the in-gate with the reins in her hand and Richard trotting beside her, running in the line of girls leading their horses, all of them nearly identical, slim hips in tight-fitting breeches, slender legs in boots only the tops of which were shiny now as their feet stirred up the dust in the ring. They ran through the soft dirt, their horses trotting beside them, different colors, different sizes, but all of a piece, coats shining, tails floating behind them, manes braided neatly along their necks. Marcy stopped in her place in the line, one in front of her, six behind her. She knew she had had a good round, but second! It was an awfully good ribbon for her first over fences, and in a stake class, too. She looked at the horses ranged behind her and spotted Delia Duncan standing in fourth place and Louise in seventh. She and Louise grinned at each other and made the thumbs up sign.

Then they were filing past a woman in a pink skirt who smiled and said congratulations as she handed out the ribbons. As in a dream Marcy left the ring, holding the red ribbon in her hand, smiling, saying thank-you when people said congratulations. Even her hand on Richard's neck felt different, floated, almost, down his neck, as she stroked the silky softness of his coat.

Chapter 23

NAT AND SHARON met them at the back gate and the four of them walked to the barn together. When they came to Louise's and Sharon's aisle they all stopped, looked down, around, anywhere except at each other, caught in that blank space where one thing has not quite ended and the other has not yet begun. The light was shading off into the pale of evening, no longer day, not yet night.

"Well," Louise said at last, "time to pack up, I reckon."

"Yeah . . ."

"I guess . . ."

"Well . . ."

Marcy flipped the end of Richard's reins back and forth in her hand. Nat scraped a half moon in the dirt with the toe of her boot. Louise scratched Willie's neck. A big six-horse rig with lights flashing rolled past them, turned the corner out onto the road leading out of the fairgrounds.

"In Italy they say 'ciao,' " Nat said. "It means I'll see you again—something like that. Easier than good-bye."

"Yeah, soon," Sharon said, "the Sacramento show is only three weeks away. See you all there, right?"

"Right," Nat said.

"Right," Marcy said.

Louise and Sharon headed off down their aisle and Marcy and Nat continued along the road toward their barn. Marcy stopped and turned to wave, but all she saw were the retreating backs of Sharon and Louise and Willie's rump, his tail swaying from hock to hock as he walked.

All around them people were dismantling tack rooms, packing trunks, loading trucks. Many people had already packed up and left, and the place was beginning to look deserted. Marcy was seized with sadness. She wasn't ready for this show to be over. Not yet.

At Fair Hill Farm a barn party was in progress. Big platters of cheese and cold cuts and loaves of French bread were laid out on two card tables. There was champagne in a silver bucket that someone had won and an ice chest full of soft drinks and beer.

"I'm thirsty," Nat said.

"Me too."

"Hi," Merl said when they approached. "You all like something to eat? Drink? Help yourselves."

Nat took two cans of soda from the ice chest and handed one to Marcy.

"Say," Merl said, "aren't you Marcy Connolly?"

Marcy nodded and popped the top off of her 7-Up.

"Nice horse," he said, giving Richard the look. "Good ride this afternoon."

"Thanks," Marcy said, smiling inside and outside. She was amazed. Even though she knew that when she was in the ring the announcer called her number and her name and Richard's, she didn't think that anyone noticed, especially not someone like Merl Ellis.

Delia Duncan was standing in a group at the other end of the table. When she saw Marcy and Nat she smiled and waved.

"Well," Nat said to Merl, "thanks for the drinks. I guess we'd better get going now."

"See you in Sacramento," he called as they headed down the aisle.

"Righto," Nat said.

"Did you see that?" Marcy asked. "Did you see Delia Duncan, Miss Stuck-Up herself, actually smile and wave at us?"

"I saw."

"I don't get it. This whole show she's acted like I don't even exist and now . . ."

"It's 'cause you got second, 'cause we were talking to Merl. You're Somebody, Marce."

For the rest of the way back to the barn Marcy was so busy savoring this thought that she forgot something else. She forgot that Nat had told Sharon and Louise and Merl that she would see them in Sacramento. How could she see them in Sacramento if she was in Hawaii?

WHEN THEY TURNED into their aisle Marcy's parents and Jim and Sasha were clustered at the end, standing outside the tack room, their figures silhouetted by the lowering sun.

"Where have you been?" Sasha asked. "It's time we started packing."

"Saying goodbye," Marcy said, "Sharon . . . Louise . . ." She couldn't finish, waved her hand vaguely in the direction of the ring. "I'm so . . . so *tired*." She was surprised at the sound of her voice—sort of choky and thick.

"I'll bet you are," her mother said. "Won't it be nice to be home in your own bed?"

"Yeah, I guess."

"Well, we're all ready to go," her father said. "Coming, Marce?"

"I can't," Marcy said. "I've got wrap Richard and help pack up. I've got to see Richard safely home."

Sasha smiled at her. "Now that's the mark of a real horse person. Putting her horse's well-being before her own."

The six of them stood clustered in a knot at the end of their aisle, making small talk for a few minutes longer. Finally no one could think of anything else to say, and after a few last hugs all the way around, Jim and Marcy's parents drove off. Marcy stood waving, even after their car had disappeared, feeling another wave of sadness at this further proof that the day was ending; the show was over. But there was still work to be done, and she walked back to the tack room to help Nat and Sasha with the packing.

Sasha unscrewed the bridle racks and saddle trees from the wall. Marcy and Nat began packing the tack trunk with blankets and bridles, martingales and saddle pads.

"What did you mean about Sacramento?" Marcy asked.

"Huh?"

"What you said to Sharon about Sacramento. How can you ride there?"

"Why shouldn't she?" Sasha asked. "It's the next show."

"But you're going to be in Hawaii," Marcy said to Nat.

Sasha stopped in the midst of coiling up the longe line. "*What*? What did you say?"

"Hawaii," Marcy said, "with . . . with her dad. Right, Nat?"

Nat bent over the tack trunk, suddenly very busy.

Sasha put down the longe line and marched over to Nat. She took her head in her hands and pulled it up, trying to look into her eyes. "Hawaii? What in the world?"

Nat avoided looking at her mother as long as she could. Finally she lifted her eyes, then burst into tears. "It seemed all right at the time," she hiccuped.

Sasha let her arms drop and looked from Nat to Marcy in exasperation. "I wish someone would tell me what's going on," she said.

Now it was Marcy's turn to get busy. She took her hairbrush and bobby pins and hair net and stuffed them into her hatbox, then stood holding the hatbox, trying to think of something to do with it. She was as confused as Sasha. Why was Sasha so surprised? Surely she knew that Nat was going to visit her father.

"Will you enlighten me, please?" Sasha asked.

Marcy looked at Nat, but she had her head in her hands and seemed incapable of doing anything but sob.

"Well," Marcy began at last, "I thought Nat was going to spend the summer in Hawaii. With . . . with . . . her dad on his boat. And . . . and . . . I was going to take care of Joey for her. At least that's what she *said*."

Swearing, Sasha whirled to face Nat. "What possessed you to make up a cock-and-bull story like that?"

"I don't know," Nat wailed. "Jim . . . Oh, what's the use?" She got up and started out of the tack room, but Sasha grabbed her arm.

"You can't run away from this," she said. "You owe me an explanation. And Marcy."

"Last . . . last winter," Nat managed to say, "when you were being so lovey-dovey with Jim I . . . I . . . decided to . . . to . . ."

"Run away? Split? Take off? Abandon ship?"

Nat winced at the word "ship." "Uh-huh. So I told Marcy I was going to stay with my dad on his boat."

"In Hawaii?"

Nat nodded.

Sasha made a sound in her throat, something between disbelief and understanding.

"You mean it's not true?" Marcy asked incredulously. "You just *made it up*?"

Nat nodded.

"You mean you never talked to your father? He never wrote you about the coconuts and the fair winds?"

Nat nodded, looking thoroughly miserable. "I wrote him, but he never wrote me back. He . . . he—" she broke off, sobbing again.

"Of course, he didn't," Sasha said. "Hawaii, my foot."

"He doesn't live in Hawaii? He doesn't have a boat?"

Nat shook her head and mumbled something about Kansas City and a taxi cab.

Marcy gaped. Even though she'd hated the thought of Nat going off on the boat with her father, it was an image she had firmly entrenched in her mind. Now she had to replace it with this person who lived in Kansas City and drove a taxi. "But why? Why did you lie to me?"

"I don't know," Nat mumbled. "I . . . It . . . At the time . . ." She went on like that, starting sentences, then breaking them off.

Sasha put her arms around her. "Nat, Nat, as bad as that?"

"Oh motherrr," she wailed, then started crying again. Sasha held her and stroked her back, while Marcy watched, unable to believe what she was seeing and hearing. She'd *never* heard Nat call her mother anything but Sasha.

"But why?" Marcy asked.

"I . . . I . . . I don't know. It just made me feel better. And then—" Nat paused and took a deep breath, "When you believed it, I started believing it too."

Sasha said, "Well, I can understand that. Sometimes people need to do things like that to protect themselves."

Nat nodded, but Marcy started shivering so hard her teeth chattered.

"Marce, I didn't mean to hurt you! I really didn't. I was so miserable myself I couldn't think of anything else. Any*one* else."

Marcy sank to the floor, feeling absolutely drained.

"And then it got so I was so ashamed of myself that I couldn't tell you," Nat said.

"Well, now I know," Marcy said bitterly. She kicked at the wall in disgust. "Some friend you turned out to be!"

MARCY WRAPPED RICHARD'S legs and helped with the packing, feeling as if she were underwater, it was so hard to move. Even the most ordinary action took conscious effort. "Okay," she'd tell herself, "pick up the wrap." She picked up the wrap. "Now wind it around Richard's leg." She wound it around his leg, pulling it tight, first with her left hand, then with her right. In this manner, giving herself instructions, she managed to finish packing and get Richard ready for the trip home.

When the truck was packed, Sasha went to hitch up. Then they loaded the horses into the trailer and headed toward the gate of the fairgrounds. Their headlights picked up bits of trash skittering along the deserted aisles, a stall door creaking in the wind. It was hard to believe that only hours before the whole place had been teeming with activity. It was hard to believe that only a few hours before Marcy had trotted into the ring with Richard, feeling utterly happy.

Beside her Nat stared ahead into the darkness. Marcy shifted closer to the door, to make as much distance as possible between them. Like an ark the truck moved through the darkness, wrapped in its own sounds of motor hum and tire swish. Soothed by the sameness of the sounds Marcy let her head loll onto the back of the seat as she watched the road unwinding before them through half-open eyes.

Pictures unrolled before her like the billboards they passed in the night: Richard standing in the muddy paddock out at Foggy Greek Stables; Richard snorting and prancing the day she brought him home; Richard, transformed, as she led him from the ring that afternoon, holding the red ribbon in her hand. *Click, click, click.* More pictures. Random scenes from the show: the teeming crowd in the schooling ring; a bunch of girls in boots and breeches gathered at the concessions stand; a braider perched on a ladder, holding a piece of yarn in her teeth; Nat grasping Marcy's hand as they went through their good luck ritual; Nat sleeping beside her, her blond hair spread in a pale fan on the pillow; Nat beaming, hugging her when she emerged from the ring on Richard. Nat, Nat, Nat. She couldn't get the camera of her mind's eye to move on to any other subject.

Then she remembered something Sasha had said that evening, which Marcy had scarcely heard at the time, she'd been so hurt and angry: "Sometimes people need to do things like that to protect themselves." Nat had spun the lie like a cocoon, making a safe enclosure to wrap herself in. "You have a mother and a father," she'd said to Marcy that day last winter. "A family. You don't know what it's like to have your life be in flux all the time."

Nat was right. Marcy's family was always there, and they loved her, Marcy realized now, even if she wasn't going to be a pianist or a ballet dancer. They loved her for herself, as much as they loved Dana. No matter how miserable she was, she'd never had to weave a tapestry of lies to create a safe place for herself.

Marcy glanced at Nat. She was slumped in the seat with her hands lying loose and open in her lap, making her look somehow vulnerable and defenseless. Marcy touched Nat's cheek.

"Nat," she whispered.

Nat turned and looked at her, her eyes shining with tears.

"I'm sorry about your father."

"You're not mad at me?" Nat asked.

"Not any more. I understand—I think. Something you had to do . . ."

Nat sighed and shifted in the seat. "Anyway," she said, "I'm sure he's not as nice as Jim."

"Yeah."

"And now we'll be able to ride all summer long," Nat said.

"Go up to the water district,"

"And out to Point Reyes."

"And to the Sacramento show—"

"To Monterey,"

"And Bakersfield,"

"Santa Barbara . . ."

Tired as they were, they started chattering, suddenly excited about the upcoming shows and the long days of summer stretching before them. Gradually, their talk dwindled back into whispers and then lapsed into silence, a comfortable one this time, as the truck and trailer sped on through the night, heading for home.